Paul M. Rosenberg
410 - 653 - 2909
LAKE DRIVE

From Howard   12/15/2016

LAKE DRIVE

JERRY BAER

ACKNOWLEDGEMENTS

This book could not have been written without the help and encouragement of many people. To begin with, I'd like to thank Janet Rudolph who invited me to her mystery book group at her home to sit and listen to the best of the mystery writers. She then introduced me to Sue Trowbridge, whose expertise and patience in formatting this book was essential.

My dear friend Nancy Day, who took my original amateur manuscript and edited it and taught me how to use the correct program to type it up.

All three of my children, Laura, Sheila and Joel read, critiqued and in one case edited the entire book for the 14th time. I should have realized how important punctuation and grammar were!

To the City of Baltimore with all its problems, I still love you.

I am dedicating this book to my wife of 54 years, Mikki, whose love I could not do without.

CHAPTER 1

It's never totally quiet in Baltimore. Tonight was no exception as Terry Klein and his partner, sergeant Brian Murphy, patrolled downtown in their police car. Brian had mentored Terry when he first joined the police force. They had become friends although they were ten years apart in age and centuries apart in experience. They both heard the call over the car radio.

"Gun fire at the corner of Eutaw Place and North Avenue. Robbery suspects firing at police. All available officers approach with care. Suspects using automatic weapons."

Terry and Brian were just one mile away. "Let's cut through Druid Hill Park and come in the back way down Eutaw Place," Brian said.

Terry cut the wheel, pulled a U-turn, and pressed down on the gas. Terry and Brian heard the shots before they arrived at their destination. As they turned the corner onto Eutaw Place, bullets struck their car. The car skidded to a stop. Murphy turned off the engine and jumped out of the car, gun in hand and headed for cover behind another police car just to his right. Terry was a split second behind him and, as he exited the car, was hit in the ankle by one of the bullets. He went down, falling behind the open car door to protect himself from further harm.

As the bullets bounced off the car door, Terry lay still, hoping that no more shots found him. His wound was bleeding onto the street from the shot he had taken, but with all the bullets being fired, he was afraid to lean over to see how badly he was hurt.

The shooters, using heavy automatic weapons, were keeping the police busy. Brian, caught in the gunfight, could not see that Terry was hit and still in danger.

Terry who was laying on the other side of the cruiser knew that with the racket of gunfire, no one would be coming to his aid any time soon.

But he could hear the calls for additional assistance over his police scanner. They were asking for a couple sharp shooters to take out the two men hiding behind a wall in front of an abandoned house. He hoped the shooting would stop so he could bend over and see how badly he was shot. He knew it was bad because it hurt like hell and he had no feeling in his foot. He was getting cold even with his flack jacket on.

Suddenly an enormous blast rang out and the shooting intensified. Minutes later, the shooting stopped, replaced by almost total silence. Terry heard someone running over to the car and heard Brian yelling "officer down!" As Brian reached Terry, he examined the wound and took out his handkerchief and tied it around Terry's ankle to try and stop the bleeding. Then he took off his jacket and placed it over Terry and said, "Just take it easy buddy, help is on the way."

"Did they kill the bastards?" Terry asked.

"I think one of them is dead, another has a couple bullets in him, but I think he'll survive long enough to go to trial."

With their sirens blazing the ambulance pulled along side Terry and two EMTs jumped out. One looked at Terry's ankle and called his partner over. "Let's get him to the ER right now. We have a bleeder and need help with the removal of what's left of the shoe. Let's not take a chance of removing the shoe until the doctors look at it."

Terry, having lost a lot blood, was beginning to feel a little woozy. The two EMTs brought a stretcher out and lifted Terry quickly onto it. Once in the ambulance, one of the EMTs gave Terry a shot and put an IV into his arm, while the other jumped into the front of the vehicle and drove to the ER.

Brian hopped into the police car and followed them to the hospital. Once in the hospital they rolled Terry into the ER. By this time, he was feeling very little pain because of the shot the EMT had given him. He heard the doctor leaning over him and saying, "Operating room, *now*." He wondered why, since it was just his ankle that was shot.

He watched the ceiling lights fly by as they wheeled him along the corridor. He watched nurses pass by him into the operating room, saw the mask being placed over his face, and then he remembered nothing.

CHAPTER 2

Meanwhile, just two miles from the gun fight, where the robbery had taken place, a crowd was beginning to form around the police cars and the dead robber in the street. Unlike his two accomplices, he didn't make it to the getaway car. At first it was just curiosity that brought the crowd there, but then the young gang members arrived and began to chant "police brutality" and tried to rile up the crowd. They surrounded the police cars and pushed the crowd forward, yelling abusive words at the officers, who responded by calling for support. The situation escalated into bottles being thrown and rubber bullets being shot. It did not take more than an hour for the neighborhood to be involved into a full blown riot. By evening, stores were being broken into and set on fire. The Mayor and her staff called in all off-duty officers to try and control the crowd and stop the destruction of their city. Several hours later, the Governor was called to see if he could give them some help as well. The local TV stations were all covering the fires, but were aware that they were vulnerable to being shot by some of the young gang-members who were systematically breaking into stores and emptying them out. Unfortunately, many of the stores were owned by their own neighbors, who would ultimately be affected most by these gangs.

By the end of the evening, when curfew was in place, two dozen people had been arrested and four officers wounded. Four city blocks were partially or totally destroyed and the fires had leveled five large retail stores.

The morning local TV news showed Mayor Janet Russell walking the neighborhood, talking about the need to keep calm, and placing the responsibility of the outburst directly on the local gangs. She spoke, passionately, about the need for everyone in the surrounding neighborhood to help stop the violence, and join in to help rebuild the community.

CHAPTER 3

Terry woke up with a terrible thirst. His mouth felt like someone had vacuumed all the saliva out of it, and he was groggy. He moved his head to see where he was and noticed that he was in the hospital, and there was a nurse standing next to him holding the cross that hung around her neck. "Is she praying over me? Am I dying?" he thought. He tried to speak but only a noise seemed to come out of his throat.

However, the nurse noticed that he was awake, put the cross back into her uniform blouse, and left the room. Terry let his head clear a bit and looked around for some way to get attention. He noticed a control button hanging next to the bed and grabbed it and pushed it over and over. A nurse came rushing in followed by a doctor in surgical gown.

The nurse checked the drip hooked to Terry's arm and asked, "Would you like some water?" Because he was having trouble getting the correct words out, he just nodded yes.

The nurse brought over a plastic bottle with a straw and

placed it in his mouth. After a couple quick sips, his throat seemed to clear up enough for him to say, "Am I dying?"

"What?" asked the doctor.

"A nurse was just in here and had a cross in her hand and I thought she was giving me the last rights or something."

The doctor responded, "First, you're not dying. Second, whomever that nurse was, she should not have been in your room to begin with, and I will personally have that checked out," looking over at the nurse who had entered the room with him. She just shrugged and left the room to find out who that nurse might have been.

The doctor pulled a chair over and sat down next to Terry so that Terry had to turn his head to look at him.

"Terry, do you remember what happened out there this afternoon?"

"Gunfire as I got out of the car, and I caught one in the ankle that sent me sprawling next to our car. Luckily, the door protected me from any additional gun fire, but I'll tell you Doc, that one was enough. It hurt like hell."

"Terry, you're a cop. You know that bad things happen to good people, so I don't need to sugar coat this. When we got you on the table, and removed your shoe, we realized that the bullet had shattered your ankle. There was no way any of us thought we could repair it, certainly not in a way that you would be able to walk on it. Your partner, Brian, was there and we asked him to get in touch with your next of kin to make the decision as to what to do. He told us that he was the next of kin, that your parents were gone, and you had no other relatives. He said he had been given your power of attorney.

Consequently, we thoroughly explained what the choices were, and that we needed a decision right away—while you were still under on the operating table.

"What sort of decision? What did you do? What have you done to my ankle?"

"We took your leg, Terry. About mid-calf, so that you'll have no trouble wearing a prosthetic, and getting around just as if you had two legs."

"You what? Oh shit!" Leaning forward as much as he could, he saw the empty space where his foot should have been.

"Terry, it's not the end of the world. You're alive. And there are plenty of opportunities in the police department for you to still have a very active career. At your age, and with the new designs in prosthetics, in no time you'll be able to do all the things you did on two legs, including running and skiing, if that's what you want to do."

Terry put his hands over his face and cried. He turned to look at the doctor.

"Fuck you, fuck you and fuck that prick Brian for letting you do this to me. I'll never be a cop again and you know it. You've fucking ruined my life. You're sitting there telling me that it's not the end of my life, but it is. Shit, suppose you lost one of your fucking hands and someone tells you 'Oh don't worry, we can get you a job in the hospital as an orderly.' How the hell would you feel? Just get the fuck out of here. God dammit."

"Terry..." the doctor begins.

"Don't Terry me, just get out, NOW!" he yells.

The doctor pushed the chair back, stood up and said, "I'll have a nurse look in on you, try to get some rest. I'll be back."

As soon as the doctor walked out of the room Terry leaned forward as much as possible and pulled the blanket away from his leg. Seeing the bandaged stump, he laid back and cried.

On the streets of Baltimore, another kind of chaos was occurring. The gangs who had joined in the riots, had faced off with each other for territory and spoils. They quickly designated their turf, and told their families that it was important to keep the other gangs from encroaching. Thus began gang wars that would cause hundreds of deaths over the next couple years. Mostly young black and Hispanic kids in their teens, who had access to as many guns as they needed in their neighborhoods. The loss of life in the police department added to the tragedy.

CHAPTER 4

———~~~———

Terry's rehabilitation was painful. At first, he refused to use a prosthetic. But, once they fit him correctly, he saw that this was a better option than crawling around, or using crutches or a wheel chair. That still didn't make it better, just more passable.

What got him through was Lorcet, the wonder drug. One pill and he was capable of withstanding the rigors of walking on the swollen stump. In addition, his leg required two additional operations to get the flap of the skin long enough to cover the entire wound, and be out of the way, so that the prosthetic didn't rub against the stitched area. Each time they returned him to his room after an operation, he would look down at his stump to see how much more the surgeons had taken off his leg. He was beyond simple depression, and refused to see anyone, including Brian. The staff at the hospital understood, and kept their distance. They could assist him with the rehabilitation of his body, but not his mind. A number of times it was suggested to him to talk to a psychologist. The doctors who gave him the prescription for the meds told him that they were addictive, and warned him to be careful. However, given the choice between the pain and the pills, his decision was simply to ignore the doctors' advice.

By the time he arrived back home several months later, he had decided to apply for disability. With his service record, his lawyer was able to get him seventy-five percent of his pay for the rest of his life. Along with that, he was able to use the VA hospital to get the rehab he needed and, most importantly, continue to get his meds.

When, months after his last operation the VA doctors told him he had to cut back on the pills, he instead turned to alcohol to ease the pain.

CHAPTER 5

The banging on the door woke him up. The TV was still on. He picked up the remote control and turned up the volume, so it would make the banging disappear, but the banging continued, even louder. He heard Brian's voice over the sound of the TV, and tried to tune him out, but he was persistent.

"I'm counting to ten, then I'm kicking the door down, so make a choice. Ten, nine, eight..."

Terry knew Brian well enough that he grabbed his crutches and staggered over to the front door. After opening the door, he hopped back to the sofa, threw his crutches to the side, and sat down. "What the hell do you want?" he asked Brian, without looking directly at him.

Brian looked around, walked over to the TV, turned it off, and said, "Nice seeing you too, you fucking loser! You look like shit, and your home smells like a toilet. I'll bet your parents would have been really proud of you now."

"You leave them out of this," yelled Terry.

"Leave them out of this? Are you kidding me? They worked their asses off to buy this home, and worked hard to see to it you had a decent place to live, and you're treating it like a garbage dump. Your old man would have thrown you out on your ass by now, and you know it. It's been six months since you were shot. You haven't answered any of my calls. I just can't believe you're living like this."

"Well, if you don't like what you see, just get the hell out of here. You're the one who caused me to lose this leg, and now you're Mr. High and Mighty, telling me to get over it. I have my disability pay, and I'm doing fine."

"You asshole. Some gangbanger shot you. Not me, not the doctors, not anyone else."

"I don't want to hear your shit."

"Personally, Terry, I don't give a damn what you want to hear. Sally and I were worried about you, wondering if you were still alive. I didn't know what to expect when I got here. To tell you the truth, I was happy hearing the TV when I approached your door. Look at you. You've lost a ton of weight and you're living like a bum, with garbage all over the place. Have you eaten anything other than pizza in the last six months? You're 25 years old and you're a quitter, a loser. I've never seen anything like it. I always thought you were one tough Jew. Instead, I'm looking at a pathetic wimp who can't get out of his own way. I'm ashamed of you, and I'm disappointed."

Staring directly at Terry he said, "You were the best partner I ever had. What a waste. Look around you for Christ's sake. Look at this room. Is this what you want? I don't believe it, not for a minute. When was the last time you showered? Jesus Terry, get a life! Sally and I have been waiting for a call from you for months. You do have friends, you know."

Terry wanted to respond, but the words wouldn't come, so he sat there in silence and tried not to say something stupid.

Finally, Brian stood up, walked over to the TV, turned it on, then turned back to look directly at Terry.

"When you get your shit together, give me a call," and he was out the door.

Terry sat there numb, confused. High from the beer and drugs, he looked around the room and began to think about what Brian had said. Brian had been like a father to him, and he realized now just how much he missed him and Sally. He picked up the can of beer sitting on the floor next to the sofa, drank it, looked at it, and tossed the empty at the TV.

CHAPTER 6

The next day, when Terry awakened on the sofa and slowly opened his eyes, the smell of the room and his clothes overwhelmed him, and he gagged. Knowing that any second he was going to throw up last night's binge, he rolled off the sofa, and crawled to the bathroom just in time to shove his head into the toilet. After vomiting last night's drinks, he was too weak to crawl back to the sofa, so he leaned against the bathtub, closed his eyes, and tried to think when was the last time he had brushed his teeth. He laughed at the thought. He thought about Brian's visit. Was it just last night? What time is it? Jesus, I'm a fucking mess. Brian's right, I'm just a pathetic drunk.

If only I hadn't stepped out of the car when I did. Maybe the bullet would have missed me. He looked down at his left leg or what remained of his left leg and thought, "that fucker got ten years for shooting a cop, will probably be out in six, and I'm stuck with one leg forever. God, I smell bad." He turned on the water in the bathtub. "Where is the shampoo?"

Once the water is the temperature he wants and while the room begins to fog up, he strips out of his sweats, swings himself over the edge of the tub, and slides into the hot, steamy water. "Jesus, that's hot." But instead of turning on the cold water to cool the tub down, he laid back into the tub and let the heat engulf him. After about ten minutes, as the water cooled down, he grabbed the shampoo and, for the first time in months, washed his hair. At first the smell makes him queasy and he's afraid he's going to throw up again. But, he stopped rubbing his head and laid back into the water, letting the water cover his head. When he sat up, he felt better, but a building headache was approaching disaster. He leaned out of the tub, opened the medicine cabinet, and took out his bottle of Lorcet. It doesn't take long for the effect of the pill to relax him.

Once the pain had subsided, he began to think about what he wanted to do next. Hard questions flew through his mind. They all added up to one conclusion, 'This shit has got to stop, now. I can't continue this way or I'm going to die." He began to cry, letting the hurt and anger flow out into the tub. Spent, he wiped his eyes, looked down at his leg, and said to himself, "you took my leg, you motherfucker, you will not take my life."

Once he had soaped his body, and scrubbed away most of the smell, he rinsed off, sat on the edge of the tub, and wiped himself dry. He looked down at the stump of his left leg and saw that the redness was gone, except around the area where the skin had been stitched over. He hadn't had his prosthetic on in months, and wasn't even sure he could use it any longer. He hopped into the bedroom, holding onto the wall to balance himself, and pulled the prosthetic out from under the bed where he had kicked it.

Terry put the sleeve over the stump, and fitted the prosthetic onto his leg. He tried to stand up, but fell back onto the bed. "This is bullshit," he thought. "I did it at the hospital and I can do it now." He got up and leaned against the wall, standing on both legs. As he looked up, he saw an image that scared the hell out of him. He was standing naked, on his prosthetic, in front of the full-length mirror on the back of the bedroom door. He is skeletal, his eyes are sunken, his face is unshaven, his hair is past his shoulders, and his once fit body is just skin and bones. He grabbed a pair of shorts out of the bureau, went back to sit on the bed, and slipped them on. Again, he stood up and walked across the bedroom, through the door, and down the hall to the front of the house.

The pain in his leg was bad but he knew that the only way he was ever going to walk right again was to keep the damned thing on as long as possible.

He sat down at the kitchen table and thought, 'I need to eat some real food. Christ, I don't remember the last good meal I've had. Fuck! If I show up anywhere looking like this, they'll have me arrested. I need a haircut and shave. Then get food for the house.' He looked around the place and realized just how right Brian had been in describing the chaos. Cleaning up the place would be last on the list.

After dressing, he went out to his car. Driving wasn't

a problem. Getting in and out was difficult. He drove into Pikesville, where he usually shopped, and parked in front of the barber shop. When he entered, the owner looked at him, got off the chair he was sitting on, and came over to give him a hand getting into the barber chair.

"Thanks, Joe." Terry said.

"What happened to you?" Joe asked

"Long story. I'll tell you about it while you cut off this mop on my head."

For the first time in months, Terry unloads the story of his disability to Joe, who had been his father's barber before he was his. Joe just listened.

After his haircut and shave, Terry looked into the mirror and saw a different person than he remembered from the last time he was here.

Joe said, "You look like a million dollars."

Terry laughed and gave Joe a fifty-dollar bill.

"Whoa, that's way too much, cowboy. You're going to need your money to help get yourself together. Pay me next time." He handed the bill back to Terry, who shook his hand and thanked him.

After completing his grocery shopping, Terry drove home, unloaded the groceries and realized just how tired he was. He went into the bedroom, lay down on the bed, and almost instantly fell asleep. When he awakened, it was dark. Looking down at his feet, he saw the two shoes sticking up and thought, what the hell, they look fine together.

CHAPTER 7

Almost a month later, after taking a walk on his new prosthetic, and stopping for a cup of coffee, Terry called Brian. The cell phone rang three times before Brian answered. Recognizing Terry's voice, Brian said, "Well, I thought you died."

"Cute, you Irish prick. How about meeting me for lunch, I'll even pick up the tab."

"You cheap Jew bastard, damn right you'll pay for lunch, and I'm starving. I'll see you around one o'clock, downtown, at Sol's."

Sol's Deli, a favorite of Terry's and Brian's, was just off Broadway, not too far from the Bay. Sol and his wife, Betty, owned the place forever, and their customers were as loyal as Marines. They had raised three children, sent them off to college, and now all three were very successful; two lawyers and a dentist.

Between the three kids there were seven grandchildren. Betty, who years ago started out as a waitress, now sat behind the cash register. After Sol was shot and killed in the restaurant, the children begged her to sell the place and relax, but she still arrived by seven-thirty every morning, except weekends.

When not at work, she spent as much time as possible with her kids and grandkids. She had a staff that adored and protected her and the restaurant, as if it was their own place.

In fact, it was theirs, since Betty treated them like family, and planned to leave the restaurant to her longtime, loyal employees. The only downside to Sol's absence was the verbal abuse the regulars received from the waiters and waitresses. "You really think that tie goes well with that shirt?" "You ordered the bagel and left half, didn't you like it?" "Didn't you sleep well last night?"

They were worse than your own mother. However, as long as he'd been going there with his Dad, and later with Brian, he'd never heard a customer complain.

Brian was waiting for Terry as he limped into the restaurant. Just as he passed Betty, she asked, "So what's with the limp?"

"Didn't Brian tell you what happened?" Terry replied.

"You mean that dumb partner of yours? I haven't seen him here in months."

"I had an accident, but I'm getting better. Thanks for asking."

"Tell that schmuck partner of yours, thanks for not telling me!"

He sat down across from Brian and said, "Betty thinks you're a schmuck for not telling her what happened to me."

Brian laughed, waved to Betty and said, "She'll get over it."

The waitress approached the table and asked, "So, you ordering or not?"

"Two coffees to start," Brian replied. "Give us a minute to look at the menu."

"The menu hasn't changed in 40 years so don't take too long. I'll be right back with your coffee." Brian looked at Terry and said, "You look better. You even shaved! I'm impressed."

"Look, I deserve your sarcasm. I've been the worst kind of asshole since the operation. I guess I just lost myself. No excuses. Every time I put the damned prosthetic on, I get pissed at the world. Whenever you called, I'd look at the number and say to myself, 'I don't need his pity. I don't want anyone feeling sorry for me.' Really dumb. It just seemed easier collecting my disability check, having pizza and beer delivered, and wallowing in my own misery. But, before you agree with what a shithead I've been, I'd like to say thanks. Oh, I don't mean for that lousy lecture you gave to me. But for not giving up on me, for remaining my friend. As you, of all people know, making friends is not my strong suit."

Brian jumps in and says, "True! But you don't have to thank me. You just needed a swift kick in the ass ...and I've always been good at doing that! By the way, you handle that leg like a pro."

"It's a new one. The old one was chaffing badly, so I went into the hospital and they fitted me with this one. Although they tell me that if I gain or lose too much weight, I'll probably need to have another fitting. It still hurts, but I'm determined to get used to it. I don't wanna be a cripple, either physically or mentally. I've done all the mourning for that leg I'm going to do; my days of sitting Shiva are over."

"So, what are you gonna do now? You know we can always find a place for you at the station," Brian asked.

Terry smiled and said, "Thanks, but I'm finished as a cop. It's time to move on while I can. I've been thinking of going in another direction. I loved college, and getting my Bachelor's degree, before I joined the force. I always wanted to continue my studies. As you know, I used the money from selling my Dad's store, after he passed away, but it's amazing how quickly that disappeared in just four years of studying, drinking, and getting laid. Luckily, I had the GI Bill money from those two years of service in the army."

Brian laughed and kidded, "I hope you didn't pay too much for getting laid!"

Smiling back at Brian, Terry joked, "You'd be surprised what those sorority girls can cost!"

They both laughed.

"So, now I have my disability check, and I believe I can get a student loan as well. I'd like to get my advanced degree at University of Maryland. I should be able to accomplish that in 2-3 years, and then I can do Counseling. It's a wonderful field. I've asked around, and found there is a great need for professionals in the child psychology field. Plus, the best thing is, I won't have to worry about someone shooting me again," Terry smiled.

"Damn, Terry, that really does sounds great! I've missed

having you as my partner, but I like this idea for you a lot . Are you going to move out to College Park?"

Terry explained, "Nope. I'm not going anywhere. The university has a downtown Baltimore campus where I can get my degree, and the cost will be much less because I can still live at home. I made a couple calls and spoke to a counselor, who looked up my undergrad record, and assured me that there would be no problem getting admitted into the program. Classes begin in just a couple months."

The waitress brought their coffee and asked, "So?"

After they ordered, Brian looked over at Terry and said, "Look, you know how Sally and I feel about you. We're not rich. But, between her work as a bookkeeper, and my officer's salary, we've managed to put a few bucks away for a rainy day. So, what I'm saying, is that if you need a few dollars now and then to hold you over, don't wait to ask."

"Jesus fucking Christ, Brian! You're amazing! I'm speechless. I ignore you, call you names, abuse you in every way I can think of, and you want to lend me money?! Your generosity is totally unbelievable. But I'll be okay, believe me..." Terry said, as he struggled to hold back the tears.

"By the way, I haven't yet asked, how is the family?"

Brian, finishing his coffee, put the cup down and said, "Bridget is 18 going on 35, and Thomas is 21 going on 40. They're the reason I have grey hair on my head. Luckily, Sally is the best wife in the world, and has kept those two in line all these years. Bridget has been seeing her childhood boyfriend, and Sally thinks he'll ask her to marry him. And

Thomas has been accepted into University of Maryland Law School."

Terry smiled, knowing that those three people were Brian's treasure, and Terry believed that made Brian a very wealthy man.

"Terry, what I want is for you to keep in touch with Sally and me. We miss having you over for dinner. I know it will be difficult picking up the phone when all you have to do is read books, write papers and get laid. But, do it anyway." Brian said.

Terry looked at him and said, "Brian, wherever I go, and no matter where I end up, you and Sally will be part of my life. And I thank God for that."

Just then, their smiling waitress dropped their lunch plates in front of them, and they smiled at each other. Then, Brian said, "Reality interrupts again."

CHAPTER 8

Getting into grad school was relatively easy compared to re-learning study habits after being away for several years. Hours in the library, and good counselors, helped to bridge the learning curve. The quiet of his home also helped.

His prosthetic no longer gave him much trouble, but he kept his Lorcet pills in his pocket for the occasional need. Luckily, Terry loved the courses and quickly became acclimated to the demands of studying and research.

At the request of Brian, he began to travel downtown into the black and Hispanic neighborhoods. He met with parents having problems with their young children who saw too much death and destruction in their lives. The children were 8 to 12 years of age, and had already seen more misery than they deserved. He was not only able to act as a guidance counselor for them but, in several instances, he took on the role of a big brother. He was always aware of how vulnerable he was down in these neighborhoods, as a white man, and carried a small gun that he kept locked in the glove compartment of his car.

The classes were small, the professors were tough but fair, and he found it engaging to meet in the evening, with a small group of like-minded students, and talk about the courses. He was a little older and more mature, but they seemed infinitely smarter. Since they were not living on campus, the group would meet at their apartments or at his home.

During his second year, his advisor began encouraging him to continue for his PhD. The field for child psychologists was growing and the need in the Baltimore area was dramatic. His counselor recommended he apply for a grant, and helped him receive a small scholarship from the University. Except for the group of students that he spent time with, he had become somewhat of a loner. He spent more time in the downtown neighborhoods than he spent at home and his computer was on late into the night, as he wrote his dissertation.

One particular Friday evening, he was studying with his group in the plush downtown apartment of one of his fellow grad students, Don Baker. Don was the son of a wealthy Baltimore family who, against his father's wishes, decided on an academic life rather than a business career. Terry liked Don, and loved the wine he served at his place when they all got together. As they were in the middle of one of their discussions, a new face appeared at the door. She quietly glided into the room and gave Don a quick kiss on the cheek. She brought her own bottle of wine with her.

Don introduced her to the five in the group. "Monica Kaminsky is a friend who's in the real estate business, and helped me find this place." She said hello, then walked into his kitchen, opened the bottle of wine, and joined them.

The rest of the evening was lost to Terry. He could not take his eyes off of her.

She was about 5'7", reddish auburn hair, green-hazel eyes, and simply the prettiest smile he'd ever seen. She, on the other hand, did not pay much attention to Terry, but instead concentrated on the conversations going on around the room.

At the end of the evening, she excused herself, and headed towards the bathroom. Terry got up from his chair and walked into the kitchen, carrying empty glasses to the sink where Don was washing them.

"Wow!" said Terry. "She gorgeous. How long have you been seeing her?"

"Oh, I don't date Monica. In fact, I'm not sure she has time for anyone. It's not like I haven't tried. We go out to dinner, on occasion, because my family knows her family, but that's about it. Actually, I think she came because I told her so much about you."

"Me? You're kidding, right?!"

"No. I don't kid, as you know. I've been telling her how impressed with you I've been. Actually, what I've told her, over the last year, was that we had this crazy ex-cop scholar in our group that limps around town working with under-privileged kids. I guess that got her curiosity going enough to join us tonight."

"Hell, she didn't even look my way."

"How do you know that?"

"Because I couldn't take my eyes off her all evening. If she had looked at me, I *might* have fallen out of my chair!"

Don laughed as Monica entered the room.

"So, what's so funny you two?"

"Terry thinks you ignored him all night."

Terry's embarrassed scowl told Don he was ready to choke him.

Monica observed, "You blush. That's nice in a man. I really wasn't ignoring you. I have been interested in meeting you, after all the accolades Don has thrown your way. He's a very discriminating guy. So, my curiosity was what brought me here...and I'm happy I came. Perhaps you have time for a coffee before going home? I have my car and can drop you off afterwards."

"Sounds wonderful! But, since I have my car downstairs, why don't I follow you?"

They said their goodbyes and headed out to the parking lot. Sitting at the curb is a new silver Audi SUV. As she opens the door, she says to Terry, "why don't you leave your car here and I'll bring you back later?"

Terry liked the idea. He carefully climbed in beside her, and she drove off.

"I feel a little awkward right now," Terry admits.

"Why?" responds Monica.

"I've never had a woman ask me out for coffee and, candidly, have never before met a woman as beautiful as you."

He was looking at her and noticed, "Now, *you're* blush-ing."

She finally responded, "I guess we both feel a little awk-ward. But a good cup of coffee should quiet that anxiety."

"I'm supposed to be the psychologist here."

"You'd be surprised how much psychology you need to sell large commercial real estate in this city."

"I thought Don said you helped him get the apartment he's in."

"Oh, I did. I've known Don almost all my life. I think our parents envisioned us as husband and wife, but that's not how it worked out. I like Don, but I have to be honest, I'm happy it didn't work out."

"You know a lot about me, what about you?" asked Terry.

"Why don't we wait until we have our coffee, and I'll give you a little background."

CHAPTER 9

———～～～———

Ten minutes later, Monica drove up to a high rise building and pulled up to the curb. Terry looked around to see where the coffee shop might be, just as the doorman ran around the front of the vehicle and opened the door for Monica.

"Are you in for the night, Miss?" he asks.

"Yes, thanks."

She left the keys with the doorman and escorted Terry through the front door, and into the elevator.

"Please don't tell me this is where you live?"

"Actually, it is. Is that OK? Besides, I make the best coffee in town."

The elevator stopped at the 26th floor. There are only two doors visible as they get off. She walks to the one on the right and unlocks the door. The lights come on automatically. She says, "One second while I turn off the alarm."

She disappears around the corner and immediately reappears.

They walk into a living room that is larger than the

home Terry lives in. The view of the Bay is spectacular. He walks around the room, looking out of all the floor-to-ceiling windows , and turns around to say something, but she'd disappeared.

"Come into the kitchen," she called.

In the kitchen he watches her fill her Krups coffee maker with water.

"Give it a couple minutes and you'll have the best coffee in town, as promised."

She goes into the refrigerator and takes out a tin and brings it over to the kitchen table, takes the top off and says, "These are also the best cookies in Baltimore".

"Please don't tell me you made these", he says after taking a bite.

"Actually, my Mom made them. You like them?"

"Like them?! Where is your Mother, I'll ask her to marry me."

Monica laughs and says, "I'll be sure to tell her."

Waiting for the coffee to brew, she sits across from Terry in the kitchen and grabs a cookie out of the tin. "I shouldn't, but I will."

"You're certainly not afraid of gaining weight?"

"Three days a week at the gym, plus a run every morning. No, I'm not afraid of gaining weight, just getting too used to these cookies. They're addictive."

"I can imagine," he says.

"So," he says, "tell me about Monica, other than she makes great coffee, and has a mother who I could marry in an instant."

Monica leans back in the chair starring, at Terry and says, "I'm your typical Jewish princess, whose father has a fortune, and grew up with a platinum spoon in my mouth. I was born and raised in Baltimore. I went to college in Los Angeles, at USC, and earned a degree in business. After graduation, I returned here and went to work in one of my father's businesses, selling and renting commercial buildings.

I was almost engaged once, didn't work, don't ask why. This September, I will be 25. I own this condo because my father wanted me to have a secure home, and he chose this building. Life for me has been pretty nice. Oh, don't get me wrong, I've had some unpleasantries in my life as well but, on balance, I can't complain. I've chosen to work in the field of commercial real estate that's dominated by men. For the first couple years that was very hard to get past, but I did. I did it without asking my father for help, although he has been incredible when it comes to common sense advice. I know he worries about me all the time, because he tells me. He also has told me he'd like me to get married and have a dozen kids."

They both laugh at that.

"My mother is an angel. Not just because she makes the best cookies in the world, but she is my best friend, and I love her to death. I have a number of friends who I run around with, when time allows, although I have to be careful because they don't have the expendable income that I do.

When Don began to talk about you about a year ago, I thought there's no one that's that perfect. However, he has continued to talk about you , and all the activities you're involved with regarding minority children, and I must be honest , I couldn't wait to come to the meeting to hear what you had to say. Ironically, you didn't talk a great deal tonight."

"I couldn't speak, because your entrance made me tongue tied. I've never experienced that before and, candidly, I didn't know how to handle the situation. I could not take my eyes off of you, really. That's what I was telling Don when you were in the bathroom."

Listen, as you probably already know from Don, I have been around. I joined the service right out of high school, then went to college, after which I joined the police force. I've kicked around a bit, and tried all the things I could without going to jail. In other words, because my parents weren't around to tell me what to do when I left home at 17, I made my own rules up for quite a while. What I'm trying, very poorly, to tell you is that I'm no Boy Scout. However, seeing you tonight walking into Don's place, totally blew my mind. The whole evening I was so jealous of him, thinking that you were his girlfriend, that I almost left early. I kept staring over at you, hoping that you'd look my way, but was too embarrassed to just begin to talk to you. You seemed to suck the air out of the room and I had a hard time breathing."

Monica has been staring at him, and smiled saying, "So, if you have enough breath left, why don't you relax and tell me more about yourself. From what Don has told me, your life has not been a bed of roses."

"Really not all that bad, actually. I'm an only child. My

parents were wonderful. My mother passed away when I was 15 years old, while I was in high school. She cooked and baked, but mostly she was my Dad's partner in their jewelry shop downtown. Maybe you heard of it, Stein's Jewelry?"

Monica said, "I don't remember seeing it, but I'd bet my Dad has. He's bought some wonderful jewelry for my Mom."

"Well anyway, after she died, it changed the world for both my Dad and me. He went to work, but came home each night looking older. Just before I graduated high school, he died. The doctor said it was a heart attack; I know for sure it was from a broken heart."

Monica reached across the table and placed her hand over his and said, "I'm so sorry."

"Thanks," responded Terry. "I miss them both a great deal. They loved each other so much that they sometimes forgot I was there. I remember once, late at night, I was awakened by loud music. I was maybe 12 or 13 years old. I walked into the front of the house and they were dancing to some wild music. At first, I was embarrassed. But then, as I stood there and watched them, I fell in love with the two of them again."

Terry stopped talking for a moment, lowering his head as if he was still seeing them. "It was a different time, in a different life. I finished high school, and joined the Army so I could get a piece of the GI Bill and afford to go to college. I also sold my Dad's business, and banked the money. After serving two years, I entered the University of Maryland and earned a B.S. in Psychology. For some unknown reason, I decided to join the Baltimore Police Department after college.

The pay was good and I had a great partner, who is still my friend, and in many ways my mentor, Brian Murphy. He and his wife, Sally, have been like parents to me. He was there when I was shot, and called for help. As you can see, I only have one remaining leg, or half a leg. The rest was taken after the shooting blew apart my ankle and foot. I'm now in my second year of grad school. And, if the money holds out, and it should, in a couple years I'll end up, at the incredibly young age of 31 or 32 , as Dr. Stein, super psychologist."

Monica smiled at him and inquired, "What then?"

"Well, I'd like to open a practice and work with children. I've been doing some work as part of my Masters program, with hard-core problem children, and it seems I'm good at it. Plus, I enjoy the challenge. It's a type of practice that doesn't make you rich, but I can make a good living, and feel wonderful at the end of the day. I don't need much. I own my home, which was left to me by my parents."

"As you can see, I'm not exactly a clothes horse. I don't gamble, but I do like a good scotch every once in the while. It was my Dad's favorite drink. So, there you have the long and short of Terry Stein's life. As you probably guessed, I'm Jewish, but have never practiced the religion. As far as I know, my parents never attended any Synagogue, so I know very little about the religion. I guess I'm just the average guy, working his way through life, in hopes that he'll find the rainbow everyone talks about."

CHAPTER 10

Terry stopped talking and looked directly at Monica, who had been staring at him while he talked. Their eyes connected across the table and his heart began to race. Monica got up from the chair. Terry assumed she was getting them the coffee that had now finished brewing but, instead, she came around the table and said, "I want you to kiss me."

Terry began to stand up, but Monica leaned down and, taking his face in her hands, kissed him. At first her lips simply touched his, but then she kissed him more urgently. He pushed himself to a standing position and, taking her in his arms, bent down and returned the kiss. He took her shoulders in his hands and looked down at her and said, "In about two seconds, this kid is not going to be able to stop the inevitable."

Instead of answering him, she took his hand and walked toward the back of the condo. They walked into her bedroom and she turned and said, "I have never done this before. Please believe me when I say that there is something that is going on between the two of us that I need to pursue. it sounds crazy, but please don't make light of it."

Terry watched her lips move and, feeling for the first time ever his heart banging against his chest, bends down and softly kisses her. His hands reach the front of her blouse and begin to unbutton it. Then, he hesitates.

"What's wrong?" says Monica.

"Monica, I think I could fall deeply in love with you in the next two minutes, but I have to make you aware of this leg of mine."

"I know all about the prosthetic," she says.

"It's not just the prosthetic. I can't do a lot of things that a normal guy can. I will never be able to do those things. Getting dressed and undressed is sometimes a challenge. I have to take off and put on this damned thing every day, and even I get pissed off at it sometimes."

She grabbed the front of his belt buckle and says, "Let's see just how much a problem it is." It wasn't a problem at all.

Afterwards, as they lay in her bed, he asks, "What now? I can't just go home and forget this evening. It's just never going to happen. If it were just up to me, I'd marry you, take you home, lock the doors and windows and stay in bed with you for the next five years."

"What a romantic you are!" says Monica, as she stares into his eyes. "Terry, I never dreamed I'd find you. I truly never imagined that I would meet the man that I wanted to spend the rest of my life with, but I believe I have. It's crazy, but I think I knew this before we met, having listened to everything Don has said about you. I don't have any doubts about where we go from here but, candidly, if I were to tell my parents that I jumped in bed with you on the first night I met you, they would probably have me committed. It's not who I am. We should take this slow. I think we both understand that something amazing just happened, and I know we both have our own commitments to handle right now. But I believe this is real, overwhelming, but wonderfully real. I know you understand that."

Then, to lighten up the situation just a bit, she smiles at him and says, "At some point, I want you to spend time with my parents, who I know will love you to death. For no other reason other than you're Jewish."

He laughed. "Some criteria."

"Well, I don't think it will be the deciding factor, but it won't hurt. In the meantime, you have classes to attend, and I have my career to build. I just need you to know that this wasn't some one-nighter. I have never felt like this with anyone before. I didn't think I'd ever find someone like you. I've been so caught up in building my business, it just never occurred to me just how much I needed someone to love. Can you understand?"

"I do understand, and I feel the same way. This is unquestionably the craziest thing that has ever happened to me, and I know tomorrow I will wake up and have to pinch myself to believe it's true. If anyone had told me I'd fall in love at first sight with the most beautiful girl in Baltimore, and that she would feel that way about me as well, I would have thought they were on drugs," he responds.

He leans over and takes her face in his hands, and slowly

kisses her. Monica responds, moving her body closer to him, and feeling his warmth as he enters her. This time he moves slowly, looking at her face as she closes her eyes, and he watches the movement of her breasts as her breath becomes shorter and shorter. She closes her arms around his neck, pulls him to her, and lets out a small cry as he releases into her.

He falls back onto the bed and says, "I know this probably is the wrong time to ask, but are you on the pill?" Monica laughs out loud. "You're right, this is a hell of a time to ask but, yes, so we can continue doing what we're doing all night."

CHAPTER 11

It takes just over three more years for Terry to earn his PhD. He credits his advisor, and the help Monica gives him with research. His final dissertation was published in a book titled, "Our Children Deserve Better." It sold well, especially to school districts around the country.

He continued his work with the inner city children and their families, who were experiencing more drug problems than they could handle. The children were caught in the middle of an on-going influx of illegal drugs, gang fights, shootings, killings and senseless carnage. This was reflected in the nightmares they had, the fear they had of going to school and, for some, the terror they felt just leaving their homes.

Although Monica understood his need to help these children, she was always aware of the danger he was in when he traveled through the gang areas at night, which he often did. He opened an office in his home, where he also saw patients that could pay for his counseling, many of whom were referred by Monica and her friends. Compared to the children in the inner city, these children had different problems but, to them, they were just as debilitating.

Between his job, and the time he spent with Monica and her parents, he felt fulfilled and happy. But, like everything in his life, he knew that this was a situation that was bound to change, simply because life always threw you curves.

Six months after he began his practice, Monica took him downtown to an office building on North Charles Street. They went into the building, and up to the 10th floor. As she led him down the short hall, they stopped in front of an office door and there, in gold letters on a brass plaque, were the words "Terrence Stein, Ph.D., Psychologist."

"Jesus, Monica, I can't afford this place."

"You haven't even seen the inside," she says.

They opened the door and walked in. Wood paneling covered the walls, and the leather chairs in the waiting room were brand new. They walked into the inner office and there was an exquisite mahogany desk, with a beautiful executive chair behind it, and two matching guest chairs similar to the ones in the outer office. The windows offered an amazing view looking down Charles Street, towards downtown.

"I love you, sweetheart," Terry finally says, "But going into bankruptcy before I even begin my practice does not seem like the logical step to take at this juncture."

"Actually, Dad insisted you have this office. His private office is up on the top floor. Since he owns the building, he is willing to let me set the rent, and I can, depending on how good you treat me, set it anyway I want."

He slowly looks around the office, turns back to her and says. "We need to get a sofa in here."

She smiles, closes the door with her foot and puts her arms around him.

"Desk tops work for me."

CHAPTER 12

Baltimore is an old port city, situated approximately in the middle of the East Coast. Every day, ships dock from around the world carrying every conceivable product, from Italian sports cars to Persian rugs. Then, there are the planes that continuously land from distant countries into Baltimore Washington or Reagan International Airports, just outside of Washington, carrying people and merchandise. And, the rail system transports people from Maine to Miami in just a couple of days. These modes of transportation, plus trucks coming from Mexico directly to the East Coast, and cars bought in Miami and driven up the coast, all had one thing in common; they can carry illegal drugs into Baltimore.

The drug problem in Baltimore, like most major cities in America, is acute. The police departments in the cities are either overwhelmed by the amount of drugs or, in many unfortunate cases, are part of the problem.

The people behind this influx of drugs vary from Afghans to Columbians, to Russians, to Mexicans, to the old fashioned Mafia Dons. They have in common more than the name drug lords. They are ruthless men and women who thrive off the world's demand for drugs, especially in America.

They are seldom captured with the drugs because of layer upon layer of intermediaries who do the work, many of whom are under the age of 16. These boys and girls, if arrested for distributing drugs, usually go to juvenile court rather than adult court, where they would face being incarcerated with hardened criminals. Thus this cadre of small-sized criminals are pervasive throughout Baltimore, as they are throughout the country.

Why do these kids resort to drug sale and distribution? Because unemployment of black and Hispanic teens is between 20-40%. There are many Baltimore families where neither the father or mother or their grandparents have ever held a full time job, and are living on welfare. That's not because they don't want to work. It is just much better for the family to get welfare than to accept a minimum wage job that would not cover their needs.

The biggest crime is that in these often poor communities, they feed off themselves. Most of the crime is in their own neighborhoods, involving crime against their own people. It is a system that is perpetuated by the wealthy businesses and importers of these drugs. It seems simple to understand. No poor black or Hispanic kid can afford to import or has the cash to pay for the tons of drugs that are distributed in America every day. Consequently, it is the businesses who handle the illegal transactions. It was once said that you could not have a paper dollar in your pocket that did not have some cocaine on it.

The families in the lower income neighborhoods live with these realities. They watch their bright-eyed youngsters turn into hardened criminals. They die from drugs and from killing each other to extend or protect their territories before they are old enough to vote.

Brian has been a witness to this travesty all his adult life, and worked hard with the inner city kids to try to get some of them out of there. He has asked Terry, after he began his practice, to work with these kids for free, if necessary, and Terry had joined him in this often exasperating battle. Every once in a while they had succeeded, which kept them in the game trying. They knew, that without the cooperation of the various factions within the city and without a place for these youngsters to get jobs, it was a lost cause. But they tried anyway.

Terry is sitting behind his new desk when Brian knocks on the door.

"Anyone home? Nice digs for a one-legged doctor."

Terry smiles at seeing Brian, gets up from his desk, walks around and gives him a hug.

"It's been too long," says Terry. "How's Sally and the kids?"

"They're great, thanks," answers Brian.

Looking around the office Brian says, "This must be Monica's idea, because you have no taste whatsoever."

"It was Monica's idea. She convinced her father, who owns this building, to work it out with his future son-in-law. At first, I was wary, but since I now do most of my business with the downtown agencies and the police department, this location is very convenient. By the way, it's good to see you Mr. new Lt..."

"Truthfully, I'm not quite used to the role yet, but I'll keep at it. Sally likes the fact that I'm inside more often and only go out after others have been to crime scenes. She also likes the extra pay. Frankly, I think she was surprised that her dumb Irish husband passed the test for the job."

"Sure," laughs Terry.

Brian says, "Well, all kidding aside, I wish you well my friend, and I do appreciate all the work you've been doing for the inner-city kids. Those children seem to respond really well to your approach. I'd love to have a dozen more of you, spread throughout the city, to work with these youngsters, but you're the only one that works this cheap," he says smiling.

"Right now I'm here on different business. Do you have a few minutes to discuss a problem that has reared its ugly head over the last few days?"

"Of course, sit down. Can I get you coffee or a cold drink?"

"I'm okay, maybe later."

"This sounds serious," says Terry.

"It is, at least I think it is, but let me explain and then you decide. There have been rumors running through several police stations around Baltimore of missing minority children. The problem is that no one has reported any missing children. With all the turmoil around Baltimore these days, we're not sure where or who might be involved or even if there is a problem. However, you can imagine, with the public's opinion of our police force right now, we need to be very careful in following up on all these rumors.

To add to the confusion, from what I hear from our different precincts, the supposedly missing children belong to some of the downtown gang leaders, and they don't trust cops. My fear is that the rumors might be true and that a major gang war is about to erupt.

The police department has every available officer out on the street trying to get information before something explodes. However, what bothers me most is, 'Why would gangs take each other's kids?' In all the years I've been a cop, when they are angry with each other, they shoot first, and ask questions later. Also, there have been zero calls about missing kids."

"Where do the rumors come from then?" asks Terry.

"The famous 'anonymous'."

"So, what can I do to help you? Right now you don't even know if the rumors are true or not. It could be that some of the gangs are sending out the rumors so they get different gangs to go to war with each other. With the recent shooting of another black kid, the entire area is on curfew. The whole story seems a little odd, does it seem that way to you?"

"That's exactly how I feel and 'odd' worries me, especially when it comes to disappearing children. Someone could have taken advantage of all the confusion that has taken place over the last week or so, but it would be unlikely that someone wouldn't have seen something. What we're getting from our people on the street is a massive stonewalling. Now, why in the hell would these parents stonewall the police if their children have gone missing?"

"The thing is, Terry, we need someone to talk to the leaders of some of these gangs. Over the last few years, through our Juvenile Division, we have sent many of these kids to you for help, just to keep them out of prison. You have seen and met a number of the parents and I thought, if you could, you'd reach out to some of them to see what you could find out. If it's just a rumor and nothing else, great. If we have a major problem going on with missing children, I want to know, and I want to know now. Because if these children are missing, you can imagine what the families are going through. If they are not sure who took these children, it could cause a great deal of injury to the innocent, and give me a migraine."

"The other possibility," says Brian, "is that some outside group is trying to create havoc in our city. That's a scenario that could get out of hand. I believe there are some families willing to open up to get to the bottom of this. Remember, these gangs are primarily made up of kids, but they have parents, or a parent, that they listen to. You think you can take this on?"

Terry says, "You know I will. I hate it when the children end up being the ones getting hurt in all this so-called gang-banger crap. I'll make a couple calls to get free from my regular patients, then take a ride downtown. I'll keep you informed if I find out anything."

Brian gets up and says, "Thanks, Terry. I really appreciate your help."

"Well, I haven't helped yet, so save the thanks for when I do. In the meantime, aren't you and Sally becoming grandparents pretty soon? It seems your daughter has been pregnant for 12 months."

Brian laughs, "More like two years. Yes, she's due soon. I'm trying to get her husband, Scott, to realize he's going to be a father and he needs to spend more time at home. Young people! I went to his shop the other day and Andrew, his brother, said that Scott had been busy elsewhere the last couple days. What could be more important than his business and his wife and future child? Shit, I sound just like my old man."

Terry laughs and says, "You're just getting old, and the young have a way of frustrating old men."

"Just wait until you and Monica tie the knot. You'll see what it's really like to be married, and then have kids that give you grey hair and heartburn. By the way, your wedding day is coming up, and Sally and I are looking forward to seeing the two of you settled down. As you know, we love Monica, and can't wait to see her march down the aisle."

"Believe me, my friend, no one is more anxious then I am. I wish it was already over."

Brian's cell phone rings and he immediately answers and listens. His face shows the concern he has for the call, and what is being said to him. Finally, he places the phone back in his pocket and says, "Sorry Terry, I've got to go. It seems one of my officers stopped a van down on North Avenue, near Callow, for going through a red light. The driver pulled a gun and shot the officer who, luckily, was wearing a vest. He'll end up with a sore chest, but he'll be okay."

"Did they catch the shooter?" asks Terry.

"Yes, just as he was trying to get to I-95, one of our cruisers spotted him and rammed him so hard that he ended up driving into a wall. Another kid with a gun. I'm telling you, Terry, it's getting worse every year."

"Why did the kid run?"

"The van was full of drugs. The gangs use these youngsters to transport the drugs knowing that if they're caught they go to juvenile detention rather than prison. They're smart and getting smarter. Oh well, at least we stopped him, and no one was killed. Gotta run! See you later, and thanks again for your help."

CHAPTER 13

Monica and her mother were on a shopping spree. They were both determined to make Monica's wedding unforgettable. It was a month before the wedding, and they both were feeling the pressure, although Monica knew that Terry didn't care at all. He had wanted to go downtown and have a judge handle the whole thing. He had no relatives, and the only names he requested to receive invitations were the Murphy family. Brian Murphy was his best man.

Monica's father, Sol Kaminsky, a real estate developer, had offered his country club for the wedding and dinner. The two women had already picked a well-known orchestra, as well as selected the flower arrangements, and had eaten a half dozen different sample dinners to make sure they had the right one – and it did not include chicken. However, they had family and friends that were vegans, that were diabetic, that were vegetarians, that were gluten intolerant and even a few that only ate steak and potatoes. As far as Monica's mother, Becky, was concerned, everyone needed to be happy at her daughter's wedding, period.

Becky asked, "So does Terry like his new office?"

"Mom, he loves it. The furniture we picked looks wonderful and very professional. He still insists on not having a secretary, but I think he'll change his mind once he gets busy. We were in the office last night hanging his diplomas on the wall. While we were working, he took me in his arms and told me how much he loved the new office, and the work I had done to get it the way he wanted. He wished his parents were still alive to enjoy the moment with us."

Her mother smiled and said, "He's such a mensch! You are so lucky."

"I love hearing that from you. I remember when I first told you about him and his having only one leg, you almost fainted. Then I told you he was working on his PhD, from the University of Maryland, and the color came back in your face. I am lucky, I adore him. I just wish he'd spend more time with his practice and less time with the clients the police department sends him. I've sent him a number of very wealthy patients. He should concentrate on them rather than gang members. With all the burning and looting downtown, these kids are destroying all the work their parents put into upgrading the neighborhood. The businesses they burned down hurt their own community more than anyone else. I know Dad has been very concerned about a number of buildings he owns there, but has told me to stay out of the area for a while. At least until things cool down."

"Talking about your father, he's taking Terry out to

lunch today. He wants Terry to come into the business and help him out. He's always complaining that he doesn't have someone to help him run his businesses. Since you made it quite clear to him that you don't want to get involved in the administration of the other businesses he has. I know he thinks the world of Terry, and wants to see if he's open to at least working part time with him for a while. That would give Terry the opportunity to learn the whole scope of what your father does, and at the same time, give your father some free time for a change."

"Mom, that's a wonderful idea. Terry admires Dad for all the accomplishments he has achieved, and probably he doesn't know the half of them. I feel certain Terry would go out of his way to help Dad in any way he could."

Becky says, "In the meantime, you and I have to get this wedding off the ground. We still haven't told the caterer what colors we want, and the dresses for the Maid of Honor and bridesmaids need to be picked out."

"Mom," says Monica, " I told you we would pick out the colors but the bridesmaid and the Maid of Honor could buy any dress they wished in that color. That way, after my wedding, they can wear those dresses again. It's just too expensive for them, to buy a dress just for the wedding. These are mostly working women and their fathers are not Sol Kaminsky. What I need most is for the two of us to cut down the number of attendees you have on your list. It's obscene, especially since Terry will only have five, and maybe six depending on how soon Bridget, Brian's daughter, has her baby. Plus I have a few friends I'm including. Your list must be over 10,000 of your and Dad's closest friends."

"Don't be such a smart aleck, it doesn't become you. Your father has many friends and business associates who would feel terrible not to be included in his only child's wedding. Don't worry, we'll get everyone seated. Why don't we pick out a color, that is appropriate for your friends, and will work for the caterer. Then we can go to the shop and try on your dress again. It has to be just right."

"OK mom, but I don't think Terry will notice how perfect it is when he tears it off me." Monica says, laughing.

CHAPTER 14

—————

Just down the street from where Monica and her mother were shopping, a different kind of event was taking place. Two young Hispanic boys, one carrying a pistol, entered a jewelry store and told the owner to hand over his cash. While the owner went behind the counter to open the cash register, the larger of the two boys smashed in the glass display, and pulled out the jewelry and watches. Quickly putting as much as he could into his pockets, he then moved toward the front door as the smaller boy, with cash and the gun still pointed at the owner, joined him. The boys dashed out of the store and around the block before the owner even had a chance to call the police. They were long gone before the police arrived.

The two boys, younger brothers of Manuel Diaz, who was a gang leader and a major problem for the Baltimore police, were back in their home before the police had an opportunity to get a clear description of them.

"They were two young Mexican kids. What can I tell

you? The little shits cleaned me out of all my cash and some very expensive jewelry. Christ, the gun was as big as the kid holding it. I wasn't even sure it was loaded, but I wasn't going to test him. He looked like he could handle that damned thing."

"I think you were wise, Mr. Jenkins. You never know just how nervous these kids are, and they do carry loaded guns. We'll put out an APB and let the street know we're looking for these kids, but I wouldn't hold my breath, if you know what I mean. I doubt they'll even try to cash the jewelry in, but just pass the stuff around to the other gang members. The cash they'll spend. Don't get me wrong, we'll keep our eyes open and maybe, just maybe, they'll try it again when we're closer, and can catch them. The other problem is, just as you mentioned, they're kids. The most we can do is put them in juvenile detention. It's the same all over Baltimore, unfortunately."

"Officer, I appreciate your honesty, but truthfully, that doesn't make me feel any safer. What I'm going to do is get a gun and keep it under the counter. If they show up again, they won't be receiving any cash from me, I guarantee it."

"I understand your frustration, but please be careful. They see a gun and they start firing, then no one wins."

When Juan and Mateo enter the house all excited, Manuel asked them where they've been. Juan quickly empties his pockets to show his big brother what they have as Mateo drops the cash on the coffee table.

"What the fuck is this?" yells Manuel.

"We robbed a jewelry store on Baltimore Street,"

answers Juan, expecting to get a pat on the back but, instead, received a quick slap across the face. Manuel grabbed the two of them by their shirts and pulled them to him.

"If you two idiots want to go out and get yourselves killed that's your fucking business, but next time don't bring that shit back into this house. What if the fucking cops followed you, or if someone took down your fucking license plate? You fools just put my whole organization in trouble. Now you take that shit and get rid of it. I mean dump it all in the Bay. I don't want that crap around here, do you understand?"

The two boys, frightened by Manuel's outburst, tell him they'll dump it right away. He lets them go and they collect the jewelry and take off.

Manuel mutters to himself, "Jesus, are they fucking stupid."

CHAPTER 15

Sol Kaminsky, whose office is just a few blocks away from his favorite restaurant, walked into The Forge like he owned the place, located in downtown Baltimore on the edge of the Bay. In fact, he is one of the owners and frequents the place often with his friends. He walked through the restaurant to the back booth that he had asked to have set aside for Terry and him. He shook hands with a half dozen people who recognized him, and then settled into the booth. The waiter asked him, "You want your scotch and soda up as usual, Mr. Kaminsky?"

"Please Steve, thank you. I'm waiting for someone. He should be here any minute."

After the drink arrived, Sol sat back and reminisced about his good fortune getting to this point in his life. It hadn't always been this comfortable. His father, Benjamin, a refugee from Poland, came to America like many others, with nothing but a dream. Sol's father was a bull of a man, standing over six feet tall and with enormous strength from working as a farm hand in Poland. He got a job in western Maryland, just off the boat, lifting the sides of barns with other young men newly arrived in the country. He met Esther, his future wife, while helping put together one of these barns. He was eighteen, she sixteen. They were married the first summer he was in America. In the beginning, she spoke just enough Polish and he spoke just enough English to tell each other that they wanted to get married and have a family. And they did, two boys. He bought a small piece of land and created a dairy farm.

After a few years the entire western Maryland cattle community was hit with the terrible hoof and mouth disease. The inspectors went through each farm and checked each cow. As it turned out one of Benjamin's cows looked like it might have the disease, so the inspectors placed it in a quarantined pen on the farm overnight, to see if they had to destroy the cow. If they did, they also would destroy all the other cows on Ben's farm, essentially closing him down.

That night, after everyone was sleeping, Ben went out to where the supposedly sick cow was being kept and took it over to his neighbor's farm, found one that looked almost the same, and brought it back to his place. His neighbor had been inspected and they had found no disease in any of his animals. The next morning when the inspectors came by and checked the cow they saw that the cow was not infected and Ben's farm was approved. Luckily the cow Ben replaced did not have the disease either. Consequently, Ben decided that this was enough of dairy farming.

He sold his farm to the neighbor, whom he had switched

cows with, and moved into downtown Baltimore where he bought a butcher shop. He spoke Polish, a little German, Yiddish, and now English, although not so well. His customers loved him since he had a wonderful sense of humor, and he knew how to treat the women.

Esther had her first child, Solomon, in 1940 just before America got into the Second World War. Three years later, as the country was in the midst of war, their second son, Abraham, was born. Baltimore became a base for the sailors during the war, with ships going in and out of the Chesapeake Bay every day. The young men who landed in Baltimore for the first time were welcomed by the nightlife along the wharf. There were whores of every color, size, and age. There were strip joints, one after the other. No one asked what age you were to buy a drink or get a whore, as long as you wore your uniform.

Baltimore prospered and so did Ben. He bought several houses along Broadway, which he rented at exorbitant rates to families of the soldiers who were relocating from the Midwest to find jobs. By the end of the war, and into the '50s, Ben accumulated a number of these row houses and became what was then becoming known as a slum lord.

Esther, however, did not fare well. She contracted diabetes and would find herself confined to her bed. The children learned to cope, since Ben was too busy to worry about them. Both Sol and Abe took after their father, and were growing very quickly. They roamed the streets looking for trouble – and sometimes found it. By the time Sol had reached his teens, he had had his nose broken four times, while Abe was smaller but, never-the-less trying to be just as tough as his older brother, found a gang of boys he began to hang out with.

When Sol turned eighteen, he tried to enlist in the army, but was rejected because of a busted eardrum in his right ear. He was devastated because he imagined that the Army would be his ticket out of Baltimore. Instead, Ben took him aside and told him he wanted him to work for him as a property manager, since his real estate business was growing, and the city was constantly on his case about fixing the buildings and bringing them up to code. At first Sol hated the idea, but soon saw that he had a knack for working with the various people that he had to hire to do the jobs, and it still gave him time to play around along the wharf at night.

Esther passed away when Sol was 20. Against Ben's wishes, Abe joined the Marines and was sent overseas. Six months later, Abe was killed in an accident. That was when Ben began to drink. He had hired people to run his butcher shop, and Sol was there to handle the real estate. Sol watched Ben turn from a happy, robust father into a drunk who could not get enough booze down his throat every day. Sol, who had been as affected by his mother's and brother's deaths as his father, could not persuade Ben to stop. In his mid-forties, Ben fell over and died from a heart attack. Sol found him in their living room, just feet from his favorite chair.

Sol had a decision to make. He was young, and could afford to take off and leave Baltimore for good if he sold everything. Instead, he became fanatic about the real estate business, and doubled the number of buildings he owned by 1985 so, at age 45, he became one of the wealthiest real estate owners in Maryland. He was on first name basis with most of the local politicians, who came to him for campaign money, and was invited to the Mayor's home several times to meet and greet out-of-town dignitaries. But, he was lonely and didn't realize just how lonely until he met Becky Goldman, an assistant bank manager. He was signing papers for a new building construction loan when she walked in and handed the final copies to the bank manager whom Sol was working with. She was about 5'6" tall, with long red hair pinned back away from her face, and hazel eyes. She smiled at him as she dropped off the papers, and left. She caught his eye and his heart. Over the next six months, she was overwhelmed by Sol. He asked her to marry him after their first date, but she put him off for as long as she could. Finally, after a walk around Druid Hill Park, he held her hand and, looking into her eyes asked, "Will you please marry me?"

Becky leaned into him and put her arms around his neck and whispered, "Yes."

They were married in the synagogue her parents belonged to. She continued to work for the bank until she became pregnant with Monica. From that point on, she became "Mom." Sol still stared at her in awe of just how beautiful she still was.

CHAPTER 16

Sol was still imagining Becky's face as Terry entered the restaurant. When Sol saw Terry walk in, he was again impressed with how confident his future son-in-law was. Sol had grown very fond of Terry and, not having a son, considered him as part of the family already. He was delighted when Terry accepted the office space. After all, who was he going to spend his money on if not his wife and only child. He had heard Terry's life story from Monica. He knew how hard Terry had worked to earn the PhD behind his name. He also knew that Terry, unlike a number of other people he knew with "degrees" had a solid head on his shoulders, was unimpressed with his degree, and loved the career he had chosen.

Terry shook hands with Sol, and took a seat in the booth. The waiter came by and Terry ordered a drink.

"So, Sol, when are you coming by to see the new office? It's really wonderful the way Monica fixed it up. Thanks again, your generosity is appreciated."

"You know it's my pleasure. Just the happiness of seeing how it made Monica feel was enough for me. I'll come by, don't worry about that. I like to see how my tenants are doing." Sol said smiling. "So how's your business?"

Terry says, " It's doing very well. With all the children of friends of Monica's, and the work I've been doing for the police department, I keep busy. Just today, my friend Brian Murphy was by and asked me to do some work for him. It seems there's a rumor that some gang children have been kidnapped or disappeared and no one has reported anything to the police. He's worried that with all the distrust the community has in the police, that they just don't want to get the police involved. The fear is that, instead, the gangs will take the problem into their own hands, and a gang war might begin."

"How can you help him? It seems that if the community won't talk to the police, they certainly won't talk to a psychologist."

"Actually, Sol, I have been working with a number of children whose parents belong to gangs. Just like their parents, they get into trouble, but the police have been sending them to me before they go into some courtroom and find themselves in the system. These are 8- to 12-year-old kids, who are really only imitating what they see on the streets. Most of them have witnessed horrible situations in their short lives, from beatings to murder. They're not bad kids, but they could end up as bad teenagers, and find themselves in prison with adult criminals. Then, we'd lose them altogether. Most of their parents, although they might be affiliated with gangs, don't seem to want their kids involved, so they've been grateful for the work I've done. What I'm going to do is call on one or two of those parents, and see if they know anything about missing children."

Sol says, "Those neighborhoods have become danger-ous for white people to walk in. You sure you're going to be OK?"

"I've been down there many times Sol. I'll be fine. But, you don't want to hear about my day. How is yours?"

Sol thought how easy it was to talk to Terry. He looked you in the eye and listened to what you had to say, and was always changing the subject to get you involved in the con-versation. He was sure most of that came from his educa-tion; however, he knew a great deal of it came from being who he was, and how his parents raised him.

Sol says, "To tell you the truth, it's been good and get-ting better all the time. I have been blessed, not just in my business, but with a wonderful wife and daughter, and now with a future son-in-law who cares about people. What could be better than that? That gets us to why I asked you to join me for lunch. You know how much Becky has been pushing me to retire, and how much I have resisted. The businesses I am involved in keep me busy and happy. In a way, I think Becky understands that but, at our ages, she thinks we should be slowing down and doing some travel-ing. She's right as usual. The problem has always been that, although I have a number of competent people working for me, I have been a one man show all these years. I know all the ins and outs of each business, whether it's commercial or retail buildings, restaurants, or even some of the interest I have in car dealerships. And, believe it or not, a few start-ups in Virginia and California. I love the action, but I would love to have someone I trust to begin to take some of the load off me, if for no other reason, to make Becky happy. You know how I feel about you and Monica getting married. You have given us such joy, that it is indescribable. We thought for a while she was going to be like her old man and spend the rest of her life involved in growing her business. When she brought you home for the first time, I could see how much love there was between the two of you, and it was like a gift from God. You know that I grew up a lot differently than Monica. My father was an immigrant and, my mother, what can I say, she was an angel, who pushed me to study and she pushed me to speak English correctly. Her constant advice was that I should never feel less than anyone else, no matter what their background, religion, or how much money they had. I remember her favorite saying 'act as if.' So I did. My father taught me how to buy and sell real estate. By the time I was 21, I was buying buildings all over Baltimore and then into the surrounding communities like Pikesville and Chevy Chase. It was easy then to expand into other cities, and different parts of the country. However, I was lonely, and my life changed one day for the better. When I met my Becky, I was already in my 40s, and she was so amazingly beautiful, the first time I saw her, I knew she was more important than the work I was doing. It took me a while to convince her, but she finally gave in and, all I can say is thank God for her. Now I want to slow down and spend my last years having fun with her. I can't give her back the years we've missed traveling, but we can now go anywhere we wish, and that's what we're going to do. However, a great deal depends on me finding that one someone that I trust to eventually take over the business. Someone smart enough, and with good instincts, to learn and handle the nuances of running many businesses successfully. I now know that I have found the person, but I don't know how he would feel about taking on this responsibility." He looks directly at Terry and says, "Terry, I would like you to consider the job. It might mean eventually giving up your psychology practice, although, I'm sure you could still handle some clientele. It would be up to you."

Terry, stunned, puts his drink down so it doesn't spill and says, "Sol, what can I say, I'm overwhelmed. I never expected this. Monica never mentioned that you were thinking of retiring, and certainly never mentioned my joining you in the business. I am literally speechless."

"First, I'm not retiring. I'm beginning the process of slowing down, that's all. Second, before I can even consider slowing down, I need someone to pick up the slack. Your involvement would facilitate that process immeasurably. Terry, I don't need an answer today. I want you to think about it and, of course, discuss it with Monica. This is very important to me, as you can imagine. It will take time to learn all the interests I'm involved in and to meet all the people that will be your supporting team, lawyers, accountants, etc. So we're not talking overnight, but, it would take a commitment. I know what kind of commitment you made to get your PhD, and I've seen how you've handled yourself since you and Monica have been together, and I believe you're the right man for this job. So, there you have it. I know you'll make the right decision. Get back to me as soon as you can. I understand it will be a considerable change in your life and your work. It will also require a great deal of your time. Please understand, I do not offer this to you lightly. I have thought about this for months. So now, let's have some lunch."

CHAPTER 17

When Terry arrived back at his apartment that evening, Monica was waiting for him with an anxious look on her face. "So tell me what you told my Dad?" "Why didn't you mention what your father had in mind? Jesus, I was speechless. You have any idea what he's handing us?"

"Mom just told me about his idea today while we were shopping. As soon as she told me, I knew it was the best decision my dad has made in a long time. When you think about it, who else would he hand it to? He loves and admires you. He knows about people, probably better than you do. He probably knew the minute he saw you that you were the man he wanted, exactly the way I did, if you remember."

"Remember, I have wet dreams about it," he answers.

Monica cracks up, gives him a big hug and kiss and says, "So, what did you tell him?"

"Actually, he told me to discuss it with you and then get back to him. I guess he saw how blown away I was by the offer and wanted me to catch my breath and talk to you. I've told you what my feelings are for your parents. They have treated me like a son since we met. It's just an enormous change. I've never even owned a business. I sold my Dad's jewelry business when I joined the army."

"Maybe that's why he likes having you. He can be your teacher and mentor, and you come with no preconceived ideas as to how to run a business. You can understand that he would not make you the offer if he didn't trust you and respect your ability."

"I get that," says Terry, "It's me. I don't know if I have the ability. Handling this level of business will be an enormous responsibility. What if I'm not capable of handling the job? What then?"

"Terry, you're a psychologist. You tell me what you'd do?"

"This is Terry Stein, the jeweler's son here, talking about handling one of the largest companies in the city. Give me a break, this is somewhat overwhelming."

"Terry, whatever you decide, I will understand and support your decision, as will my parents. They are not offering this to you because they think that's what I want. They're doing this because they think you can and will be a success at the job. In the meantime, how about taking your wife out for dinner, I'm starving?"

"I don't know how you do it. You're always hungry and you never gain weight."

"After dinner," she says, "we can come back here and I'll show you how."

CHAPTER 18

The next morning, when Terry arrives in his office, he sees an email from Brian. There are a couple names of gang leaders that he suggests Terry contact. Because of the pending wedding next month, and all the things Monica had him doing, he had eased his schedule enough that he decided to take a ride downtown to see one of the people listed. This would at least take his mind off the heavy decision he was faced with regarding Sol's offer.

Southeast Baltimore can be a tough neighborhood. And it usually is. Terry had traveled through the neighborhood many times, picking up and dropping off families that had a need for his service. Most of the families he worked with had someone that was a member of a gang. It was how they survived. He did not judge them, but tried to separate the problem area from the problem child. Most of the time this was impossible. However, every once in a while, he succeeded in pulling a youngster out of his or her mindset that the only way of life was joining a gang or using drugs. The problem these children had was that they had seen more blood of friends and family on the streets, by the time they were teenagers, than most people will see in a lifetime. So, as teens, they were already hardened to the life they lived. Most were convinced they would never reach adulthood. This was reinforced by the gangbangers who controlled the streets where most of them lived, whether black, Hispanic, or white. The gang mentality was the same, be tough and control and protect your neighborhood.

Terry drove through the neighborhood towards the house that Gladys Diaz's father owned. He had never met Manuel Diaz but, had on several occasions, met with his wife and their daughter Gladys, who began taking drugs at ten. This was enough to frighten her mother into bringing her to Terry. After many sessions, both with Gladys and her mother, he succeeded in getting her off drugs. Now she was 13 and doing well in school. Her father was a gang leader and had a reputation that kept the police on watch around his house most days. They knew he was trouble, but were unable to catch him in anything illegal, so far.

Manuel was in his 30s, a contemporary of Terry's, so Terry thought this would be a good place to begin. The one area that Terry made sure he stayed clear of was any discussion about the drugs in the neighborhood, because he knew that Manuel controlled the flow of these drugs, mainly heroin.

He wasn't sure how they received these drugs but, knew that in almost any neighborhood in the city, you could find any drug you wanted, even on school campuses. Somehow the gangs in Baltimore, whether Hispanic, black, white or Asian, had a continuous supply of drugs, including crack. Brian and the Baltimore police had tried every way they knew how to find the source, but were constantly finding themselves at a dead-end. Brian's advice to him, which he took to heart, was work with the kids and leave the rest of the problem to him and the police.

Terry parked just down the street from the house, which was covered with iron bars across all the windows, and a heavy metal door leading into the house, just like most of the other houses on the block. The homes were well kept and the street seemed like any other in this part of Baltimore.

He approached the house, walked up the steps, and rang the doorbell. A child's voice came through a small box next to the bell, "Who the fuck are you?" Terry looked up and saw a small camera pointed down at him. He looked right at it and said, "I'm here to talk to Manuel Diaz. My name is Dr. Stein."

For a full minute there was silence. Then there was the sound of locks being opened on the other side of the door. Terry faced a youngster, about 10, who looked past him and told him to come in. After the door was shut and locked, the young boy pointed at the stairs to the second floor and said, "Go."

As he reached the top of the stairs, Manuel met him. He stood about 5'7", with dark skin, and a pair of dark black eyes that stared right into him. He was a young man used to intimidating people. He was dressed in baggy pants, now popular with gangbangers around Baltimore. Most of these kids did not know that this style of droopy pants was begun in prison where the inmates did not have belts to wear.

As Terry reached the top of the stairs he looked around, and then back at Manuel, who seemed to recognize him somehow.

"What you want? You the doc that helped my Gladys?" Terry extended his hand to Manuel and said, "Yes, I hope I had something to do with your little girl getting clean, and going back to school. How is she doing these days?"

Manuel did not take Terry's hand, but turned around and walked into a small room just off the top of the stairs. Terry followed.

"Why you here, man?"

Terry, looked around and saw a chair just to his right. He said, "Do you mind if I sit down, I have a bum leg." He sits and Manuel sits across from him.

"Manuel, there have been rumors all around Baltimore that children are missing. The police are baffled, since no one is reporting these children as missing. They have asked me to check around, and see if the rumors have any validity. And, if so, to confirm who is missing, and for how long. If the rumors are wrong, great, and I'll just be on my way."

Manuel looks hard at Terry and says, "Gladys is missing. She disappeared two days ago. She knows better than to run away from home, and I have my people out there looking for her. If I find some guy is with her, he's fucking meat. You understand me?"

"Manuel, have you heard of other children in the downtown area that have gone missing?"

"Who the fuck cares about other kids. I take care of mine, let them take care of theirs. Besides, Gladys's mother thinks one of the other gangs might have taken her. If that's true, there's going to be hell to pay."

"What if I can get the police to search the downtown area and help you find her, no questions asked? They want these rumors checked out and are willing to put a lot of manpower into getting to the bottom of it, one way or another. What do you think?"

"I don't trust them. My guys will find her, believe it."

"It's your call, Manuel, it's your daughter. However, if my daughter were missing, I'd get everyone I could to help me find her. What the police are concerned about is not just your daughter, but the others as well. They want to determine whether or not some gang from outside Baltimore is trying to start a war here, by creating chaos, so they can come in and take control while everyone's preoccupied with missing children. The police can help. You should at least meet with them, or tell them that your daughter is missing. I'm going to meet with several other families and see if they have had a child disappear. If so, I think you all have to be concerned."

Terry pulled a business card out of his wallet, handed it to Manuel, and said, "Your wife may have lost my card, so here's another one. It has both my office and cell phones on it. If you want to get together, I promise it will be in confidence. Just call."

Terry gets up and limps over to the stairs.

"What happened to your leg?" asks Manuel. "I used to be a cop and got in the way of a bullet that destroyed my ankle. The doctors took my leg below the knee. It happened a long time ago but, believe it or not, sometimes I still feel the pain in that ankle. Weird, huh!"

"Fucking crazy, man."

Terry leaves the house and calls Brian. "It's not a rumor anymore. The Diaz family has been missing their little girl for two days. I'm going over to see if I can meet with Ricky Jones. His son was one of my patients. I told Diaz we wanted to help, but he says that his crew is out on the streets looking because he doesn't trust the police. I gave him my card and told him to call me if he wanted help. I'll keep you informed."

Brian says, "I'm going to send some cruisers out to the area to see if we can spot some young girl that might be in trouble. I'll tell the officers to keep their eyes open and call me if they spot something rather than approach her. I'll call you if we find anything."

Sitting in his car, talking to Brian, Terry failed to see the car speeding down the street behind him until it rushed past him. The car windows opened and several guns became immediately visible as shots rang out, ripping across the front of the Diaz house. In seconds the car turned the corner and was gone.

"What the hell was that? Are you OK?" yelled Brian into Terry's phone.

"I'm fine, but the front of the Diaz house is riddled with

bullet holes. I'm going to see if everything is okay in the house. Get a car out here forthwith ."

Terry gets out of his car and hurries over to the house, looking around to make sure the car doesn't come around again and sneak up on him. Before he can ring the bell, the door opens and Manuel and two other young men are standing there with guns in their hands.

"Is everyone okay in the house?" asks Terry.

"We okay," says one of the young men, "but nobody fucks with our house, nobody. Those assholes are dead."

"What assholes? How do you know who it was? I was outside and I didn't even get a chance to see the license plate."

"Oh, we know," says the young man.

"Shut the fuck up!" says Manuel.

"This is just the beginning," says Terry. "Someone is inciting a war that will get lots of you killed, and you still won't get your kids back unless we figure out who in the hell is responsible for taking them in the first place. Please give the police and me a chance to help," Terry pleads with Manuel.

Manuel says, "Get the fuck out of here. I need to think."

Terry leaves again, quickly gets into his car and drives away. He is worried about going to Ricky Jones, another gang leader, but decides to go there anyway, knowing this area could escalate into a war zone in short order. He thought, 'what the hell have I gotten in the middle of?' The shots had brought back his memory of the gun fight when he lost his leg, and chills went through him. He thought he was past that but realized, while driving to the next stop, how one never fully gets over that level of trauma.

Terry dials Monica's cell phone. He knows talking to her always makes him feel better and, right now, feeling better seemed like a good idea.

Monica's mother answered, "Terry, how sweet. Monica and I have been all over Baltimore getting ready for your wedding. She's in the dressing room trying on her gown. She told me that Sol finally talked to you about joining his firm. I hope you accept. I have been encouraging him to talk to you for months. He's stubborn, but I think he realizes he needs to begin to pull away from all the work he does. I know what he thinks about you, and I believe you'll be wonderful for him and his company. I hope you'll consider the offer as a mitzvah. Not just for Sol but, for me as well."

"Right now I could use a mitzvah," he laughs. "Becky, I love you and Sol and I will talk to him soon about the offer, I promise. In the meantime, give my future bride a big kiss for me and tell her I'll see her at dinner."

"I will, I promise," answers Becky.

Terry remembers that he needs to pick up his new tuxedo today. The wedding is just three weeks away. He has made reservations at the Park Lane Hotel in New York, one of Monica's favorite places, for their honeymoon. He made sure they had the honeymoon suite at a cost he couldn't believe . He had purchased theater tickets, also at obscene prices, for four shows the week they were there. Sol had helped get reservations at a number of the best restaurants in the city. Brian, his best man, had the two wedding rings.

Becky had helped him pick out the right designs. Sol had hired a limo to take them to the airport, after the dinner, and rented a private plane to fly them to and from New York. "What could go wrong?" he laughs to himself. What you didn't expect was always what came back to bite you in the ass.

CHAPTER 19

Brian Murphy is a boy scout. After almost thirty years of marriage, he still adored his wife and children. He had worked his way up the ladder of promotions through hard work, and many hours of study. He had not only mentored Terry but a dozen other officers who would give their lives for him. He is 6'2", 205 lbs., with curly salt and pepper hair, and a smile that brightens his whole face. His son, Thomas, who had recently graduated law school, was working 60-70 hours a week for a well-respected law firm in Washington, DC. His daughter, Bridget, who had made it through her teens without getting pregnant, as Brian kidded, was married to her childhood boyfriend, Scott McNary, and was due any day with Brian's first grandchild. Scott owns an auto repair shop downtown with his brother, Andrew. The shop was left to them by their late father.

Brian was parked just outside the auto shop, hoping to take Scott out to lunch. He walked into the shop and again was impressed with just how large the facility was. The auto center had grown quite a bit from when they took over the place. There were 6 mechanics working on cars, some of them police vehicles. They had added a tire center next door. They had a paint shop around the corner, and were talking about an automatic car wash. Brian liked the two boys. Now that Scott was his son-in-law he made sure, as often as possible, to spent time with him. Brian saw Andrew working on a new Honda and approached him. "How you doing, Andrew?"

"Busy," he answers. "We might need to add a couple more mechanics if business keeps growing. A great problem, huh?"

"I don't see Scott, is he around?"

"He's out with a couple of our friends talking business, as usual. That guy never stops. He should be back in an hour or two. I think they're having lunch at Mario's, in little Italy."

"I know the place. Good food. I don't think I'll bother him. I hope he has his cell phone on. The baby is due any minute."

"Are you kidding me," says Andrew. "If I hear any more about his kid, I'll scream. My mother even told him enough. Take a look at his office over there and see just how many toys that idiot has already bought. Amazing what having a child will do to you. It's one of the reasons I'm staying single."

Smiling, Brian says, "Oh, that could change in a minute, if you meet the right girl."

"I'll wait," answers Andrew.

Scott is sitting in the booth at Mario's, finishing the pasta dish he ordered and listening to Ralph, one of his childhood friends, who was now his lawyer. "It can work. The financing could be in place in a couple months. The houses we're talking about have been vacant for at least 10 years, so the price shouldn't hurt. The question is what to do with the properties. Tony, you're the only one that can tell us if we have the right location , and what best to build on them. You know the area. Your family used to live along Lake Drive."

Tony looked at Ralph, all 200 lbs. of him, in his lawyer's three-piece suit, and a watch fob hanging in front, attached to an old pocket watch his grandfather had given him for his bar mitzvah.

Ralph's family had been lawyers in Baltimore for three generations. They handled everything from criminal to patent law. Most of their income was generated by work they did for lobbyists in Washington.

As Scott once said, "Ralph will never have to worry about his next meal."

Tony Romano, who stood 5'8" in his stocking feet, was the strongest of the group. He had been doing contracting work with his family from the time he could remember. He now worked for himself and, over the last few years, had built enough of a reputation that his year was filled with jobs all around town. He had a small crew of men whom he could call to help with larger jobs, and liked the independence of working when he wanted, on jobs he liked doing. He and Scott had grown up together.

When Tony wasn't working on some job he was playing golf, which was his passion. He had taken lessons, trying to get his handicap down to 15, but so far it had remained at 18.

"It is a nice idea, Ralph, if for no other reason than we could make a good profit out of it. I believe we should put up condos on that property. However, putting up condos along Lake Drive could create some problems."

"What kind of problems?" asks Ralph.

Tony, who had been listening all this time to the proposal that Scott and Ralph had come up with, looks down at the piece of paper he'd been writing on and says, "First, we need to find out if we can build something other than single-family homes on that block. After all, that used to be a very wealthy area, and they might have restrictions for the neighborhood that have to be addressed. Second, there might be height restrictions as well. Then, we need to find out if the city, or some private person or persons, own the four houses left on the block. In other words, there are a few questions to be answered before this project can get off the ground. Don't get me wrong, none of the issues make the project insurmountable. They just need to be answered to our satisfaction. It will take me a few days to do some leg-work, and then I'll get back to you. By the way, is Andrew going to be in this with us?"

Scott says, "Absolutely."

Ralph says, "OK then, I'll file papers for a new corporation, with the four of us as partners. What do you two think we should call it? It has to sound professional, or people won't take us seriously."

Scott suggests, "How about 4 Baltimore, Inc. The number four can mean four people and, that the company is *for* Baltimore."

Tony says, "Jesus, I like that. How in the hell did you come up with that?"

"Genius," says Scott.

Tony and Ralph laugh, and then Tony says, "Scott, you're so full of shit."

Ralph says, "Let's meet at my place tomorrow night." Looking over at Scott he continues, "Bring Andrew. There will be papers to sign."

"I'll be there unless Bridget delivers our genius child tonight."

CHAPTER 20

—∿∿—

Terry finally arrives at the home of Ricky Jones. There are a half dozen youngsters out front. They are not playing games, they're guards watching the street and playing soldier. Terry parks in front of the home and is immediately surrounded by this cadre of kids. One of them, obviously the leader, steps up to the driver's side door and curtly asks, "You in the wrong fucking neighborhood?!"

"I'm here to speak to Ricky. How about telling him Dr. Stein is outside, okay?"

The youngster stares at him like he had mustard on his face and then, speaking to the others, tells them to watch over Terry while he goes into the home. Ten minutes later, while Terry sits and catches up on some of his emails, the young boy comes dashing down the stairs and tells Terry to come in. Unlike the Diaz home, Ricky's place is well-appointed. As Terry walks into the the living room, which faces the front of the home, he notices that it's full of over-stuffed chairs and a large TV set. There is a beautiful rug on the floor and artwork on the walls. Ricky invites him to sit down. Ricky, tall, thin, dressed in Levi's and a black t-shirt, and wearing expensive cowboy boots, has his long hair in a ponytail. His arms are full of tattoos. He has gold chains around his neck, and a number of bracelets on his wrists.

"So, what do I owe this visit to?" he asks.

"Let me get right to the point," says Terry. "There is a rumor that there are missing children from some of the gangs in Baltimore. That is, rumor until about an hour ago, when I found out from Manuel Diaz that his daughter is missing. We believe there are other children missing and I'm working with the police department to clear this up. I've seen first-hand what could happen if we don't find out what's going on."

Ricky sits up in his chair and says, "What do you mean, first-hand?"

"I was at the Diaz home and a car sped by shooting the place up. Luckily, this time no one was hurt, but that probably will not happen the second time around, since the Diaz family is now on full alert. What I need to know is, are there other children missing and, if so, who and for how long? The police are already out there cruising the neighborhoods to see what's going on but, without your help and the help of the other gangs, they'll get nowhere. Lt. Murphy thinks it might be an outside group trying to start a gang war here, and he is intent on not allowing that to happen. Has any child from your family disappeared in the last couple days?"

"My nephew," answers Ricky. He went missing last night, and my sister is going crazy."

"How old is he?"

"He just turned 12."

"Why in the hell hasn't she called the police?"

"You're kidding, right? He might be in some alley shot through the head by some cop right now."

"Suppose you're wrong. Suppose he is somewhere alive, and scared to death, but no one is coming after him. You just don't have the manpower the police have and, I can assure you, that Lt. Murphy is quite serious about finding out what's going on. Let me bring him into this. I can call him now and ask him to meet us here. I'll make sure he comes alone; to show you he means business. What do you have to lose?"

Ricky looks away from Terry for just a moment and says, "You tell him, I see a bunch of police cars, marked or unmarked, come into my neighborhood, there's going to be some fucking trouble like he never seen before. You get it?"

Terry calls Brian and brings him up to date. "I'll wait here for you," he says.

"I should be there in less than 30 minutes ," says Brian.

After hanging up, Terry says to Ricky, "He should be here in less than a half hour. In the meantime, is there a picture of your nephew we can have to circulate around town?"

Ricky answers, as he pulls out a cell phone, "I'll get you one." Ricky calls his sister and tells her what's happening with Terry, and then tells her that she needs to bring a picture of Kenny, her son, over to him right away.

After he hangs up, he turns to Terry and says, "My family is important to me. My sister raised me and, when she hurts, so do I. You find my nephew and we both owe you. You fuck with us, and there really will be a war."

"Ricky, when I heard about the possibility that some of your children were missing, I immediately imagined what you must be going through. Missing a child has to be the worst possible nightmare. I've known Lt. Murphy for years and, can assure you, his only concern is for the safety of the kids. Every day he faces the deaths and destruction from overdoses and murders concerning those drugs. But, he is also a father, and empathizes with the pain that comes when a child is injured, missing, or killed. If anyone in the city can help resolve how your nephew went missing, he can and will. But, having your assistance, and the assistance of the other gangs in the city, would definitely help. So, keep an open mind when he gets here, and let's work together to find an answer to your nephew's disappearance."

"Look, I'm meeting with him, ain't I? I'm not going any-where."

CHAPTER 21

After Tony finishes the decking around the home on Smith Ave., he decides to take a ride down to Lake Drive to look over the properties again. Many years ago, Lake Drive was considered one of the best neighborhoods in Baltimore, with large mansions lining the street. All of them faced the vast acreage of Druid Hill Park. The park housed a reservoir, massive outdoor swimming facility, a zoo, and hundreds of paths and thousands of acres of grass , shaded by trees. Branching out from Lake Drive were beautiful cobblestoned streets, which were lined with trees. During the '40s and '50s, you could find a fruit or vegetable wagon going up and down the street with the vendor shouting out to the neighborhood what he was carrying. The houses, single family, three-story row houses, all had large front porches where everyone congregated during the spring and summer months. There was an abundance of children, all playing along the pavement and in the streets. This was a period in Baltimore's history when the servicemen from around the country, who had frequented the strip joints on Baltimore Street along the Bay, came home as civilians. They went back to school on the GI Bill and began to build America into the industrial power it would become. Baltimore was in transition. The wealthy families, who built their mansions around the Lake Drive area, began to move away and into the suburbs. Their departure left a vacuum in the area, which was immediately filled by middle class working families, who either rented or bought these homes, and even subdivided them into apartments. As time passed, these families found the inner city hard to cope with. They too moved to the suburbs selling their homes below their value just to escape the problems of the growing crime rate.

Eventually, the houses began to fall into disrepair, and no one seemed eager to to fix them. They were boarded up, and some were burned out. The result was an entire neighborhood deserted. The city began to tear the houses down. The four mansions that Tony and his friends were considering buying on Lake Drive were standing monuments of what used to be. They were once wonderful majestic old homes, now in total disrepair, and probably would fall down with a good wind. The wood was rotted, and the foundations broken. Tony looked at them with admiration, knowing the amazing workmanship that went into the creation of the four buildings, but knew that he would have to destroy them to accomplish what he and his partners wanted to do. He had spent a couple hours down at city hall, going over the title records, and found out that the city of Baltimore now owned the property, and would be happy to sell it to anyone who would develop it and upgrade the area. He swung his truck around Druid Park, and approached the four houses, just in time to see a Good Humor truck pull out of the garage of one of the old mansions.

"That's weird," he thought as he parked. "That bastard is getting free use of a garage. It takes all kinds. Well, he's going to be pissed when I tear the places down." Tony walked the property again, trying to envision how the condos would lay out. He was not an architect, but he'd worked on enough properties to know which direction he wanted the buildings to face. He was awaiting confirmation from the city that they could go as high as 6 stories, with elevators. That would give them a hefty profit from each unit. He had already figured they could put up 36 units on the property, if they received approval. They could build twelve units per building, and have three buildings. Each unit within the building would be about 800 sq. ft. with two bedrooms and two baths. He could build them for around $105 dollars per sq. ft. or only about $84,000 per unit. However, with the demand this close to the downtown financial district, the sale price for units like that could easily sell for as high as $175,000. He liked the idea so much, he had already decided to buy one of the units for himself.

As he walked the property, he noticed that the garage that the ice cream truck had exited from had a padlock on it. This guy has some balls, he thought, but let it go as he continued to stroll through the four properties. He looked across the street from the property, at the vast expanse of grass and trees that was a part of Druid Hill Park, and could envision how the condos would eventually face that direction. He was excited, and knew the rest of the guys would be as well, once this project got under way.

CHAPTER 22

The Good Humor truck was headed downtown to pick up its supply of ice cream for the day. It was driven by Ed Teller, who had just dropped off another child into the basement of the old mansion on Lake Drive. Ed is a handsome man of 70 years, who doesn't look like the typical Good Humor truck driver. However, he was on a mission, and it was not to sell more ice cream. He was driven by hatred, and was single-minded in planning to avenge the death of his son. He did not notice, or would he have cared, that Tony's truck was parked near the house he was occupying.

Edward Teller was an accountant. He was born and raised in Baltimore and loved the city, as only a native can. He grew up just north of Druid Hill Park, off Park Heights Avenue, in a middle-class neighborhood. His parents were discontented socialists, who raised their child to look for the shortcut to success. Edward learned quickly that his parent's idea of life was not what he wanted. Consequently, he finished high school and college, getting a degree in accounting. He worked for an accounting firm that took notice of him, and his total dedication to his job, and he regularly advanced over the years. He retired as a CPA and Senior Vice President of the firm. He was quiet, unassuming, and talented in his field.

Late in life, when he was almost 53, he met and married a quiet, lovely woman, Sharon Gorski. She was 38 years old, of Polish background and, like Edward, worked very hard to advance herself professionally. Her field of purchasing allowed her to interact with vendors without getting personally involved with them socially, which she preferred.

When Edward introduced himself to her, she was considered an old maid by many of the people she worked with, although they would never tell her this to her face. She liked Edward and, if for no other reason than to quiet the rumors about her, she began to date him. Eventually, she grew to understand and love Edward, and his unassuming personality. They married and, to their surprise, Sharon became pregnant two years later. At first Edward, who did not want children, was not pleased. However, Sharon being Catholic, persuaded him that the only thing to do was have the child. She told him that they could afford to have her stay at home, and care for the child, and that's what she wanted to do.

Unfortunately, the birth was a difficult one, and Sharon found out later from her doctor that she would not be able to conceive again. She was not disappointed, since she had a healthy little boy, and she knew Edward did not want more children anyhow.

They named the boy Randolph, after his grandfather.

He was everything Sharon could have hoped for, and Edward was taken with him from day one. He was quiet, slept through the night most of the time, and had a smile that captivated Edward as much as anything he could remember. Late at night, he would hold the child for hours, just watching him sleep. Both he and Sharon held him so much that people who knew them wondered if the child could or would ever walk.

But walk he did. And run. And he grew into a typical little boy of 10. Edward and Sharon had, by this time, moved out to Stevenson, Maryland, an exclusive neighborhood, just west of Baltimore. Their beautiful home had a swimming pool, guarded by a high fence, to keep Randy safe and also keep other kids in the neighborhood out. Randy had learned to swim at an early age, but Sharon didn't trust him to be in the pool alone. He was also on a little league soccer team, although he was not very good at soccer. He was not much of a team player, his coach told Sharon. But she didn't care.

One day, after school, she told Randy that she was going to take him downtown later, to meet his father, and go out to dinner together. She told him to shower and she would lay out an outfit for him. Excitedly, he ran upstairs into his room. He was dressed and ready for their adventure before Sharon arrived downstairs. They climbed into their Cadillac, pulled out of the driveway, and drove downtown.

After she parked the car in the garage, below Edward's office, she took Randy's hand and said, "Since we're early, let's take a walk up Charles Street and look at some of the stores, okay?"

Randy took her hand and followed her. Over the years, Sharon had gained a taste for fine jewelry. She had her favorite shops that she frequented, but was always looking for something new. She stopped in front of a jeweler's window display and Randy, seeing a toy shop just a couple doors away, walked over to look in their window. As Randy stood there, two cars approached the corner where they were standing. As they drove by, the car windows opened, and gun shots flashed. The two cars drove away as fast as they had arrived. The window next to Sharon had exploded, frightening her, but leaving her unharmed. She looked around for Randy, and saw him leaning against the wall of the toy store, his clothes covered in blood. She screamed, ran over to him, and held him.

People from the nearby stores came running out. They saw Sharon and Randy but, there was little any of them could do. The police and an ambulance arrived at the same time. Randy was dead, and Sharon was in a state of shock, from which she would never recover.

For the next year, Edward had Sharon in and out of psychiatric institutions, with the best doctors money could buy, but to no avail. Finally, Edward unable to cope any longer, placed Sharon in a home where she received 24-hour nursing care. Her private room was decorated as nicely as her own bedroom. Edward saw to every detail. The doctors said she might eventually come out of the mental state she was in but, after a year of therapy, Edward held no hope.

Instead, he went to his lawyer and set up a trust fund with more than enough money to take care of her for the rest of her life, however long that might be. He retired from the firm, he went back to his home with single focus and began to map out a plan; a plan of revenge. The killers took his life away from him, now he was going to make someone pay. The police had never discovered who had committed the shooting, or why, although they believed it was gang related, which did not surprise Edward. Therefore, he intended to seek his own justice.

The plan was simple. His plan would take time and patience, and he had both. An eye for an eye. His child was gone, his son. Now there would be a price to pay. The gangs that killed him would pay. He wanted them to understand the pain that occurs when someone takes their child from them.

His plan came together one day, when he was perusing the ad section of the Baltimore Sun, and he saw a notice for the sale of a used Good Humor truck by someone in Pennsylvania. Edward flew to Philadelphia and met with the man selling the old truck. After inspecting the truck, he negotiated a price with the owner and drove it back into Baltimore, to a downtown warehouse that he had leased. There, he carefully cleaned the truck and set about creating a false floor, just inside the door. He soundproofed the small space and put a lock on the trap door. He then ordered a Good Humor man uniform and contracted with a local ice cream manufacturer to purchase ice cream, and all the other equipment he would require. He bought a license from the city, to sell ice cream from his truck, and had a city inspector come out to give him his approval. He had the truck repainted with a new sign, "Henry's Ice Cream" with colorful balloon stickers pasted around the sign.

Once spring arrived, he traveled through the inner city, selling ice cream in the various neighborhoods, until he felt he knew every route in and out of the area. By summer, his plan was taking form. He saw the children on a regular basis, they felt comfortable with him. The parents were not bothered by another ice cream truck in the neighborhood. He was ready to put his plan into effect.

Edward had searched around for a quiet neighborhood where he could take and hide the children. He wanted it far away from the inner city, but not near his home. He found just what he wanted on Lake Drive. There were four abandoned homes, which were boarded up, but had garages attached to each. He went there late one night and, using a pair of pliers, opened one of the garages. It was large enough to fit his truck and, of those homes, was in the best condition. He closed the garage door, then went to the back of the home and looked for an easy access point. He did not want to be visible from the street. He saw a basement door, which he opened to look inside. The place smelled of mildew but, using his flashlight, he entered. There were no lights, so he scanned the room and saw that, once he cleaned out the cobwebs and put out rodent traps, it would work for what he had in mind. It also had a number of small windows, which he realized needed to be covered.

Over the next week he painted all the windows in the

basement black, brought in a large battery-operated light fixture, and cleaned out the room. Once satisfied, he placed a lock on the basement and garage doors. He was ready.

CHAPTER 23

Terry, Brian and Ricky stood around in Ricky's living room. Brian introduced himself and handed Ricky his card. Ricky looked at the card and put it into his pants pocket. "So, what you going to do to get my nephew back?"

"Do you have a picture of your nephew?" asked Brian.

"Here" he said, handing the picture to Brian, that his sister, who was sitting quietly on a chair, had brought over to him.

Brian stared at the picture, then at Ricky's sister, and said, "He's a good looking boy." Then, looking back to Ricky, he continued, "I'll have his picture circulated today all over the city. If he's wandering around somewhere, we'll find him." Ricky interrupted, "Suppose some other fucking gang took him? Suppose they're trying to get even with me, or someone in my family?"

"Ricky," replied, Brian, "I've been a cop for 30 years, and I've never seen a gang kidnap a kid from another gang. It's more likely, if they were pissed off at you, they'd come by shooting. Isn't that right?"

"Yeah, but this could be the first time."

"It could, but we know that several children have disappeared from the inner city gangs, and that doesn't make sense. It has everyone in the force worried that some outside group might be trying to start a war in our city, and we are all working this case as of today. Rest assured, by tonight, every cop available will be on this. That's why Terry suggested we get together. My manpower and resources are much greater than yours and, hopefully, we can get this resolved very soon, for all of our sakes. You have my card, please have your people call me if they find anything. We're setting up a command center just a few blocks from here, and I will have cruisers stationed there just in case something develops. I'm heading to the homes of several other families in this area to express to them exactly what I just told you. We need everyone's cooperation if we're going to solve this quickly. Can I count on you, Ricky?"

Ricky, about to tell him to just do his job, hears his sister sob, turns to Brian and says, "Get it done. You find out where my nephew is."

"We're going to do our best," says Brian, as he and Terry head for the front door.

Outside, Brian says to Terry. "You've been an enormous help Terry, thanks. I think we can handle the rest of it, so go home and give a hug to Monica for me."

"This kidnapping has me confused, Brian. Gangs, as you mentioned, don't kidnap each other's kids. These gangs are focused on drugs, not kidnapping. And, if they're angry, they come with guns, and someone usually gets killed. If it were some group outside Baltimore, then they would make it clear they were here and, again, come with guns blazing. If some outsiders wanted to create a war here, I would think they'd pick just one child from any one of the families and tell the others, so they'd create the war they want. However, taking children from each family makes no sense."

"So what do you think is the cause of the disappearances?"

"Just off the top of my head, I'd say someone is pissed off at the gangs. Maybe it's one of their drug suppliers. Possibly they short-changed them and they are getting even by holding the kids until they get paid. I don't know, except, gang warfare just seems far-fetched. I'll have to think about it some more and get back to you. The one thing I know is, your involvement will help keep the lid on any killings, and that's the best that can happen right now. You're a good cop, old man."

Smiling back at Terry, Brian says, "Thanks, now get your ass home and I'll be in touch."

CHAPTER 24

"Can you believe the wedding is only a few weeks away?" asks Monica.

"You wanted a June wedding, I just wanted a June bride," said Terry.

They were sitting in a seafood restaurant, around the corner from Terry's office, having dinner. The weather had been getting nicer each day. Terry had a taste for crab cakes so, even though the official season was over, they ended up here at Graffeo's. "God, these crab cakes are good," said Terry.

"Don't make a pig of yourself. Take one of them home. They're enormous."

"That's a good idea," he answered.

"So, did you and your Mom have fun getting your wedding gown fitted?"

"We always have a good time together. She's fun to be with and, more fun when she picks up all the checks. You know my mom. She wants everything to be perfect for her daughter's wedding, even though she knows perfection is impossible. Which reminds me, did you get your tux fitted? God forbid you should look like a shlump on our wedding day. Terry laughs at her use of the yiddish word and says, "I will look as good as possible, but standing next to you, anyone would look like a shlump."

Terry smiles and continues, "What I can't wait for is to have you walk around the apartment naked, and not feeling guilty about watching you."

Monica smiles and says, "Enough, or we might not make it back to my apartment. Now, please tell me you spent your day thinking about my father's offer?"

"Not every minute, but I have given it a great deal of thought. I'll try to meet with Sol tomorrow, if I get the opportunity, and get some questions answered."

"What kinds of questions?"

"Well, first of all, what is my position with the company going to be? What kind of salary is he talking about? Where will I have an office? Who will I be reporting to, and who will report to me? And, some other less significant, but important, questions that keep popping up in my head. There is also a nagging concern I have that Sol feels I can handle the job, and I personally have some hesitancy about that. So, I want to spend some time with your Dad and get clarity around what he wants. This is not an easy decision for me, sweetheart. But, believe me, I will make every effort to see if the job he's offering is a good fit for me. I have to feel confident that it's particularly right for me, and not just right for your father. I don't want to take it and find out that I got the job only because I'm his future son-in-law."

"He would never place you in a position that he didn't think you could handle. And he *definitely* wouldn't take you into the firm just because you're my fiancé. Believe me, I know my father."

"I'm sure you're right but, let me meet with him and work out the details. I want the time with him anyway, okay?"

"Tomorrow for sure, promise me."

Terry stares at Monica, knowing her stubborn streak is showing, and says, "Alright, I'll see if he's available tomorrow to get together, okay?"

Still smiling, she reaches out to touch his hand and says, "I knew you'd see it my way."

CHAPTER 25

———❧———

Ralph is in his office, with Tony and Scott sitting across from him. Tony has told them about the property, and what it looks like. He says to them, "The city is willing to sell us the whole block for $100 per lot. Right now, they consider the whole area blighted. They would also waive certain ordinances, that were put in place 60 years ago, regarding single family homes. However, they are requiring us to upgrade the sewage, to accommodate the number of units we want to place on the four lots. They have also conceded that having 5 or 6 story condos there would not impede the view of anyone, so I think we can go forward with finding a good architect to put the plans together."

"First things first," says Ralph. "We're now incorporated, as of yesterday. We have an account with Baltimore Financial Bank, just around the corner from here. They have given me temporary checks for our account. They said the printed checks would be here in a week or two. I'll take a check down to City Hall and buy the properties, so they are in our company's name, then begin the process of doing all the paperwork. We don't want to get ahead of ourselves. In the meantime, Tony, do you know an architect that would look at the property, and make suggestions, before we start incurring big fees? If we don't like the guy, we can look for someone else who is more creative. Okay?"

"Actually, I know someone. She's a beautiful young woman, whom I've been seeing off and on for a few months, who can help us. She works for an architectural firm. I'll touch base with her tonight, and get back to you two with her advice."

"So, tell me," asks Scott, "What's she like, and just how serious is this?"

"She's really terrific," answers Tony. "She's from Virginia, and graduated from the University of Virginia four years ago. The reason she came up to Baltimore for this job was because her Dad, who is a builder in Alexandria, got her an interview. That's how I met her. She came out to one of the jobs I was working on, to get me to sign some papers my client had given to her firm for my approval. I told her I'd sign off on the blueprints if she would have coffee with me. Her name is Janet Douglas, but she goes by JD."

"Jesus," says Ralph, "That's the most unromantic approach to dating I've ever heard. Besides, you're lucky she didn't have you thrown off the job for sexual harassment." Tony laughs.

"You don't understand. She had previously seen me on the job site, and wanted to meet me. So, she volunteered to bring the paperwork out to me, rather than have a courier do it. She wants to become an architect. However, from what she tells me, it takes a great deal of time, patience, and doing the crap work before she can apply. I like her. She's honest, and has a couple dimples that I just want to climb into."

Scott and Ralph laughed and Scott says, "Sounds serious, my friend. Why don't you have her meet us here, or at a restaurant, to discuss ideas. That way we can all meet her."

"Since the two of you are happily married, I don't see a problem with that. I'll set it up," Scott says. "I'd better get back to the shop, and tell Andrew what's happening. Once he gets his head under the hood of a car, he's lost. I wish some cute single girl would bring her car into his shop and fall for him. He's so caught up in the business, he doesn't have any social life. I tell him to take some weekends off, and head to the Eastern shore or up to New York for some R&R, but he's so happy doing what he does, he doesn't pay me any attention."

Ralph says, "Hell, he's still young, leave him alone. He'll be okay."

"He's my brother, and I worry about him. If he isn't fixing someone else's car, he spends his weekends rebuilding that old Corvette convertible of his. It must have three hundred coats of wax on it. What girl wants to sit around while her husband is polishing his car every weekend?"

Ralph says again, "Just leave him alone. He'll be fine."

Tony jumps in, "By the way, some guy is using one of the garages on Lake Drive to house his Good Humor truck. I won't say anything to him until we are ready to demolish the homes. I'll put a sign on the door of the garage a couple weeks before we begin."

"He might lose his 'good humor,'" says Scott, laughing.

CHAPTER 26

───∽∽∽───

Gang leaders Ricky, Manuel and Pat Riley are standing in the middle of a large empty lot in south Baltimore. The place was a used car lot before one of the riots, in that part of town, burned so many of the cars that the dealership closed down the place, and leveled the building. They stood, surrounded by a dozen cars, with members of each of their families in each. All loaded and ready for battle. The three leaders stood together because Ricky had called them, and asked for a meeting. He explained the reason being that his child was missing, and he had heard from the police that others were also missing. He wanted to get together to see if the other families were looking outside of Baltimore for the reason for these disappearances.

"Look," says Manuel, "my kid don't go with anyone. She was fucking snatched. I want to know who the fuck did it. If this is some outside gang, why don't they fucking say something. My people are on the streets all day and night, and I can't figure out how she disappeared. Someone must have seen something. If a fucking strange car drives through my neighborhood, I know it right now."

"I have fifty people working every corner in my neighborhood," says Ricky. "There is no way someone takes a kid off the street without someone telling me, yet my son is missing. So, what the fuck?! My kid disappeared right after dinner." Snapping his fingers, he says, "Plus, as long as the cops are floating around my neighborhood, I can't get any deliveries."

Manuel and Pat shake their heads, acknowledging the problem.

"Nobody hears nothing, nobody sees nothing. It's fucking weird. And there are so many police cars patrolling my neighborhood, my business is down 50%." Ricky says, "Listen, if there is an outside family trying to stir up a war between us, we need to find out who and why. I don't want no fucking war, and I don't think the two of you do either. So, what I suggest is that we keep in touch with each other until we figure out what the fuck is going on. Manuel is good to talk to the cops and he can call us if they find anything. In the meantime, tell your families to keep their eyes open, and not let any kid go out alone for a while. As my mom used to say, better safe, than sorry. The one thing we don't want is for someone to get shot for no reason, if you hear me."

"I hear you," says Pat. "Do you know of any other kids that have disappeared downtown?"

"I don't, but Manuel can ask Murphy, and see if they

have. If so, one of us should contact the family and tell them what we are doing."

Pat says to Manuel, "Call me on my cell if Murphy has other families involved, and I'll make contact."

They stand there for a second, then Manuel says, "If I find the motherfucker first, he's dead."

CHAPTER 27

In an old warehouse in east Baltimore, Jeff Berger is focusing on the latest shipment of drugs, due in from South America in a few days. His concern is that the warehouse is beginning to fill up, and the local gangs have not taken their supplies for several days. This is a major concern. He's been involved with the drug cartel in Columbia for over 25 years, and has never experienced the magnitude of problems he's had lately. Normally, this warehouse is busy almost all day long with kids coming from all the various gang-related families, to pick up what they need for distribution into their own neighborhoods. Now it's quiet, deadly quiet.

Jeff needs the families to continue to buy his product, for which they pay cash, so he can pay back the cartel for their shipment last month. He is into them for almost $20 million right now, and the new shipment will deplete all his cash reserves. Whatever is creating this problem cannot continue. He's worked too hard for too many years, and fought too many battles, to let this get away from him.

He remembers as a 17 year-old, at Baltimore City College, getting into marijuana and, as a jock, how easy it was to get whenever he wanted it, as long as he had the cash. Standing 6'3" and weighing 235 lbs., he was looked up to even by his fellow jocks, so they were his best customers for the weed, once he decided to make some money. The easy money led him to expand his sales across the road to Eastern High. This eventually led him to an office on North Avenue, where he was forcibly escorted by three mean-looking black men, who picked him up after football practice. One of them shoved a gun in his side, and led him to their car. They blind-folded him, and told him to keep quiet while they drove.

When they arrived at their destination, and removed his blindfold, he was face-to-face with Johnny Sisk, who he discovered controlled a large part of the drug business in Baltimore. Johnny was very unhappy with Jeff's infringement in his territory. Jeff was a bully, but he was also an A student, and quickly realized he was in the home of the man who could make him rich, if he played his cards right. So rather than show his fear, which would have been the norm for most 17 year-old kids, he sat down across from Sisk, and listened to him threaten to kill him if he didn't back away from selling drugs in the school. He looked at Sisk, and didn't see how dangerous he was, but how in control he was. He was not a large man, sitting behind his desk. He was probably about 5' 9" or so, and had a slim body. He wore dark glasses, which hid his eyes from Jeff. Jeff waited until he stopped yelling at him, paused a beat, and then quietly asked, "Did you have any business at City College before I began to sell there?"

"Why the fuck should I tell you, you prick?!"

"I'll tell you why," says Jeff. "I began selling just a few months ago, and half the jocks in the school are buying from me, and I set the price I want. That tells me that there is no other place in the school they could get the weed. Now, I'm assuming that the product that I was buying and selling to the jocks was yours, otherwise, how would you know I was selling it. So, let's be honest and good business people here. I can sell your product, which I am buying at a very high price, and still making a profit. I could do the same at other schools, with their jocks, and make even more money. Now, if you're pissed that I've expanded your distribution, just tell me, and I'll back off."

Johnny starred at the kid, then at his three body guards and sat back in his chair. He said, "You have some fucking pair of balls kid, I got to say that."

Jeff interrupts, "Johnny, I apologize if I've messed with your business, but in truth, look at me. I'm a big bad white kid with a good reputation. I can get into places, with all due respect, the four of you couldn't get into with a ticket, if you know what I mean. All I would want was better pricing, and a good supply. I believe this could benefit all of us, what do you think?"

"I think I should have my boys take you the fuck out to the wharf, tie a cement block to your feet, and toss your ass in for a swim, that's what I think. But, I like you. You ain't the regular dumbshit I see here all the time, and I could use someone like you. So, I'll tell you what you're going to do. You're going to pay me $10,000 for the shit you've cost me , and then I'll sell you weed at a reduced price. However, I will expect you to sell $10,000 worth every month, or we call it quits, and I mean 'quits,' if you get me."

Jeff pauses for a second, knowing that he needs to show some business sense. Understanding that Sisk has all the power, he negotiates, "I don't have $10,000, and couldn't raise it if I tried. So, how about I owe you the $10,000 and you give me $20,000 worth of weed, at a reduced price, and I give you 50% of all the profit. Then, after I sell that, you give me what I need, at the reduced price, and let's see how much I can sell for you. You can't lose, and I can only expand your business in areas that you aren't covering."

Sisk laughs out loud, and his enforcers join in, not even knowing why. "Boy, you are something," Sisk finally says. "I'll tell you what I'm going to do. I'll give you $10,000 worth of weed and you will give me $15,000 back. Once you show me you can do this, I'll sell you, at the wholesale price, as much as you can afford. Cash up front. But let me say this just once, you fuck with me, and you will be the sorriest fucker in the world, you get that?"

"Done," says Jeff, as he gets up and extends his hand to Johnny, who takes it and laughs, "Son, you've got to have some black in you somewhere, to walk around with the balls you have."

Jeff was a natural for this business. He kept his word to Sisk, and religiously paid him back, and bought only from him. He built his territory, and it didn't take him long to realize he didn't need Sisk any longer.

That was 25 years ago. Today his life was considerably different. The warehouse Jeff had been using for his drugs had been an auto parts distribution center, in Baltimore and Washington, for 35 years. He bought it when he realized he needed to have a cover for all the shipments he was receiving from all over the world. It had been a long and difficult road. First selling marijuana, then coke and heroin, and then crack, and now added to the stew, pills.

Johnny was good to his word. However, once Jeff recognized that he didn't need him any longer, he made a plan. He had been selling drugs for him, and now it was time for him to eliminate the middlemen.   Jeff anonymously called the police, and told them that a shipment of marijuana was coming across the Mexican border, and who was getting it. Two of the Sisk brothers were caught by the Mexican police. Johnny blamed the cartel, and ranted to them about the possibility that they had a leak in their organization. He was furious, and told them to get his brothers out of the Mexican jail right away, or else.

The next day, Jeff was approached by a man, representing the cartel, who said the cartel wanted Jeff to take control of the operation. Jeff told him, as long as Johnny was in control, that was impossible. The man explained to Jeff that the problem with Johnny was he had a big mouth, and that he would be silenced by the end of the day. While the two of them spoke, five armed men walked into Johnny's offices and killed all three of the men there, including Johnny.

Then, they put the bodies into their van, and carried them out to the Bay. They were enclosed into steel barrels, and dumped into the water.

With the help of the cartel, and his own ingenuity, it took Jeff just a few weeks to reinstate the product distribution, and begin his own operation. He was just 23 when he became a millionaire for the first time. He had accounts at 10 different banks, as well as large safety deposit boxes. He no longer sold the product directly, but set up a network of ghetto kids who were spread out all over Baltimore. As the years passed, these kids grew up, and became gangs with their own territories. This was Jeff's bloodline and, now the blood had stopped flowing. Jeff called his warehouse manager over to him and suggested he call some of the gangs, and tell them they needed to do their pickups, or he was going to cut them off. If that didn't get them motivated, nothing would.

CHAPTER 28

Sol's office space, several floors above Terry's, was a contrast to what Monica had furnished for him, quite stark. It was large, with windows facing the Bay, the desk and chairs made from something other than leather, and the walls were hung with spectacular contemporary artwork. Unlike Terry's desk, Sol's was clean of all paperwork, with the exception of a large calendar book, opened to today's date. Sol was drinking his coffee, as Terry came in.

"Good morning, Sol."

"It is, isn't it? Would you like a cup of coffee?"

Terry answered, "Yes, I can fix it myself." He walks over to the back of the room, where Sol has his coffee machine, and pours himself a cup. After he sits down, he says, "I'm sure you understand how difficult a decision this is for me Sol. I'm a simple guy. I worked my way through college. I come from a middle class family. And, I met and fell in love with the most extraordinary woman, who, surprisingly, wants to marry me. And now, your proposal is thrown into the mix. I'm sure you can imagine just how overwhelming this is for me. There are so many changes."

Sol smiles and says, "She is extraordinary, my daughter, I'm glad you see that too. Becky and I are extremely proud of how she has handled her life, and doubly pleased that she wants to share it with you. You know that, don't you?"

"Yes, I do," he answered.

"Sol, if you will accept this as coming from the heart, I'd like to explain just what my thoughts are."

"Please, go ahead."

"This opportunity you're handing me is beyond anything anyone has ever done for me. I understand that you're not doing this just because Monica and I are getting married, but I also understand that if I weren't marrying her, this job would not be presented to me. I'm also realistic enough to appreciate what this offer is, and how much it means, not just to me but to you, Becky, and of course, Monica. So, I'd like to lay my cards on the table and ask you to make me a promise, if I take this position."

"Anything, what would you like?"

"It's not what I'd like, but what you need to be clear with me about. Assuming I take this job, and assuming in a few months you see that it's not working the way you imagined it would, I need your promise that you will tell me face-to-face. No harm, no foul. I'm a big boy, and I kind of know what my abilities are, and this whole proposition scares the hell out of me."

Truthfully, Terry, this has everything to do with you marrying Monica. For the first time in my adult life, I feel totally happy about the future. You did that." Raising his hand, to stop Terry from speaking, he continues, "What a parent wants most for his children, is that they be happy. You've made Monica extremely happy. I have never seen her glow the way she does when she speaks about you. There is nothing I wouldn't do for her. However, if and when you begin to work with me, and you notice I didn't say, work *for* me, then you will be engaged in daily education in not only real estate, but finance, contracts, litigation and, of course, politics. It will not happen in six months, or possibly six years. However, I have every confidence that you will be a wonderful partner for me and eventually be able to run this organization. Terry, you would be doing a Mitzvah, do you understand? As much as I have dreamed of Monica becoming a wife, and hopefully a mother, I have also dreamed that she would meet someone like you, whom I already feel is part of the family. Someone I can trust. I need to trust the person who is my partner, and who will follow me in managing the businesses I have created. I have felt this trust in you from the first day Monica brought you home to us. So, Terry, are you ready to take this on, because if you are, there are a number of things that have to be accomplished with my lawyers?"

"Sol, the answer is yes. Yes, because I can't think of a single reason not to and, yes, because it would be an honor to work with you, and I mean that. I hold you in great esteem and, if I can be half the businessman that you are, I will have achieved far more than I ever thought I would."

Sol stands up, and extends his hand to Terry, "Mazel

tov! I've already had the lawyers draw up the paperwork. So, all you have to do is run down the block to their office and sign them. Once you sign them, you'll be a partner. It will give you a substantial equity interest in the company, along with a number of other perks, including credit cards and a checking account, to draw on as needed. You and I will be spending a lot of time together, learning about each other and, please understand, if you have questions, or don't agree with what I have said or done, jump in and tell me. As much as I believe I'm perfect, Becky will tell you I'm not. But let's not get ahead of ourselves. See the lawyers, and take care of business first. Then, come back and let's have lunch, and we'll begin on the details."

After Terry leaves, Sol gets on the phone to Becky, "So, we now have a partner, and I think we should consider that cruise you mentioned for later this year."

Becky began to cry.

CHAPTER 29

Making his plan, and following up on it, was creating an unexpected problem for Ed. He wasn't able to sleep, and his appetite had diminished. He was talking to himself, and forgetting to shower, or brush his teeth. He was thinking about this, as he sat alone with the small bodies laid out in the basement of the house on Lake Drive. The most recent having been added last evening, when a little boy of around 8 or 9 came up to the truck alone, and asked him for an ice cream cone. The child pulled out of his pants pocket a crumpled dollar bill, and handed it to Ed. Ed looked around and, seeing no one around, suggested the child climb into the truck to pick the flavor he wanted. The child became very excited, and immediately jumped into the truck. Ed closed the door, got the drugged ice cream from the freezer, and gave it to the boy, who downed it in less than a minute. The boy tried to understand what was happening to him but it was too late. Ed waited until the boy collapsed, and placed a plastic bag over his head. He then quickly opened the false bottom of the cab, and dropped the dead child into it. Ringing his bell one more time, he took off, out of the neighborhood, to drop off the body.

In the basement of the house on Lake Drive, Ed had wrapped each child in plastic and, above each, he has painted the word "Revenge" and pinned a copy of a picture of his wife and son to their clothes.

He was exhausted, and he realized that it's just a matter of time before the authorities caught him, but he didn't care anymore. He wanted this finished. All he could think of now was driving back to his home, taking a hot shower, and going to bed. He'd lost weight. His appetite has all but gone, except for occasional junk food.

He remembered the delicious meals Sharon, who is now vegetating in an institution, used to cook for him and their son Randy. He thinks to himself, as tired as he is, that he owes her and his son one more body.

CHAPTER 30

When he meets Terry, later that morning, Brian is still on cloud nine after visiting his new granddaughter. As they are having coffee, Brian shows Terry the picture of the baby he took with his cell phone. "She's a doll. She looks just like her mom," Brian says, looking again at the picture.

"Yes, I think you're right," he continues.

"So, I received a call from Manuel Diaz. He met with two other gang leaders, who lost their children, and they're organizing families throughout the whole downtown and eastern Baltimore corridor to watch for any one that doesn't belong in the neighborhood. If they don't begin shooting people for no reason, this could be very helpful. I explained to him that they should report these strangers to us, before they go off half-cocked and hurt someone who is innocent. This is the first time the various families have come to us, which is a very good sign. I hope, once we clear this up, the cooperation continues. It would be nice if this crisis could evolve into something constructive for the kids downtown. I've been trying to get the city to build a facility for them in that neighborhood for years, but all I hear is, 'we have no money.' Anyway, I wanted to talk to you about a project that Scott, and his brother Andrew, are involved in. Maybe you or Monica can help them out."

"You know if we can, we will. I have some news for you as well."

"Good news, I hope."

"The best I have right now," Terry answers.

"So tell me."

"Monica's father, as you know, is a very successful businessman."

"I knew that."

"Well, he's offered to take me into the business as a partner."

"You're kidding? That's great! I can't imagine you selling real estate. Isn't that where he does most of his business?"

"Candidly, I'm not quite sure where he does most of his business. He wants to meet this afternoon for lunch, and begin to explain to me just what his businesses are. Since he wants me to eventually run them, that would be the first step."

"Wow and double wow. I'm going to have a gazillionaire friend."

Terry smiles, and says, "Look, this is all between you and me. We've known each other a long time, and I wanted you to know. The details are going to be worked out. I just came from the lawyer's office, signing papers that would place me on the corporation board, but I don't know what the hell that means, as yet."

"Terry, whatever you do, I know you'll do it well. Congratulations. What does Monica think about this? Are you going to be stepping on her toes?"

"Not at all. She's known about Sol's intentions for a while, and has encouraged me to accept his offer. She likes the real estate business, and just wants to stay with that. She told Sol she didn't want to run the business, from an office, a long time ago."

"Well that will change, once you two have 3 or 4 kids."

Terry laughs and says, "You're getting way ahead of yourself, my friend. First, we need to get married. Which brings me to the point. Have you been fitted for that tux yet? After all, you're my best man, and you need to look classy."

"Oh. I'll look classy alright. By the way, I have the rings locked up in my safe. But, what I wanted to mention to you is what Scott was involved with."

Terry says, "Right, I'm sorry I cut you off."

"That's OK. I can always use good news, and Sally will be delighted to hear about your new position."

"Remember, just Sally. I don't want this going out to the rest of the world."

"OK," responds Brian..

"Anyway, Scott and Andrew, and a couple of their pals, have purchased some buildings along Lake Drive, and are going to tear them down and build condos. The new corporation, '4 Baltimore,' does have a professional ring to it, right? One of the partners is Scott's friend, Ralph, who's a lawyer, and another friend is a contractor, so they seem to have all the bases covered. The city is giving them financial help because the Lake Drive neighborhood is so run down. I remember stories about how great that neighborhood used to be."

"Me too," agreed Terry, "It used to be a Jewish neighborhood in the '40s and '50s. Then, they all moved out to the suburbs and voila, it went downhill."

"You Jews have to learn to stay in one place for a while," jokes Brian.

"Cute," responds Terry. Then continues, "It does sound like a good idea. If they pull it off, they could probably get more properties down there for practically nothing. The problem is that once the big developers see that the area is changing, they'll want in, and the prices will go up."

"So, you think Monica can give them a hand and some advice?"

"Absolutely. I'll talk to her after lunch, and have her call Scott. She'll want to call with a mazel tov anyway."

CHAPTER 31

An hour later, Sol and Terry are having lunch together at Sol's country club. The restaurant is situated at the end of the larger of the two golf courses, which the club operates. Sitting by the window, you can watch the golfers finish on the eighteenth hole.

As they get their beverages, they watch a foursome of well-dressed women on the 18th hole. They obviously are pleased with their scores, and they walk off the green in time for the next group to approach.

"Becky sends her love," says Sol. "She's already booking vacation cruises for us."

"Really?" says Terry.

"Absolutely," responds Sol. "She's been trying to get me on a cruise ship for years, but I've been too busy to go. Now, she feels we'll finally have time to enjoy ourselves, away from Baltimore."

"Sounds good to me."

Sol takes his briefcase off the chair next to him and

opens it, taking out a large folder. "In here," he says, "are the details of the businesses you and I will be visiting over the next few months. I assume the best time to start would be after the wedding, since Becky tells me that I shouldn't bother you about it until after the honeymoon."

"I signed the papers this morning so, now that I'm a partner, I now know who the real boss is. She's an amazing woman."

"Now you know the secret of my success. The details of the businesses are not important to know right away. However, the information in the folder will at least give you an idea of the scope of what I have going. At some point, you'll get to know all the important people but, candidly, right now it's just a pleasure to know you're on board. You have made this old man very happy today."

"You're not old. The 70s are the new 40s, they tell me."

"Don't let them fool you. 70 is 70. But, thank God, my doctors tell me I could live another 20 years or more, if I take care of myself. Now I can."

"I hope so. I hope that everything you've envisioned will come to pass. Plus, I have a new project for my future bride."

"What kind of project?"

"You remember Brian, my old partner and best friend? Well, his son-in-law, Scott, has come up with a terrific idea of building condos along Lake Drive. The area has been run down, for as long as I can remember, and yet it's a hop and a skip from downtown and the Bay. Scott, and three of his buddies, formed a corporation and already purchased four houses along the street. They have an architect lined up, and have been given the green light from the city, which wants to clean up that whole neighborhood."

"Where are they getting their financing?"

"I have no idea, except Brian mentioned a bank, I think it was Baltimore Financial, where they opened an account to start the project. I guess they hope to get them to finance the loan."

"Interesting. Check it out with Monica, maybe she can work a deal with the bank. She handles loans all the time, for major projects, through many different banks."

"Good idea. I'm talk to Monica tonight and, again, thanks for everything. I hope that, shortly, you'll feel enough confidence in me, that you and Becky will take a trip around the world."

"Let's not get carried away. Baltimore is just fine with me. It's Becky who wants the cruise experience. If we like it, who knows."

CHAPTER 32

Brian had been up all night in the hospital, awaiting his granddaughter's birth. Mother and daughter were fine; however, he was exhausted. Although, he was lifted from his fatigue by his discussion with Terry. He now needed to turn his attention back to his job. He was meeting at the downtown control center, with a group of officers who, like him, are very concerned about the disappearance of children. They were all veterans of the gang wars that had, at one time or other, taken the lives of gang members as well as their fellow officers.

"Bring me up to date," asked Brian.

One by one they gave their reports, emphasizing how many officers were on overtime, to make sure all neighborhoods were covered. The reports included how many crimes had been averted, due to police presence, when calls were coming in about burglaries and assaults. However, none of the reports included anything new on the missing children, and that's where Brian began.

"OK, we have kids missing. We have no witnesses in areas where there are just too many people around for someone not to have noticed something. We have questioned the neighbors, and many of the kids on the corners and, even with their cooperation, no news. It's been three days. My belief is that this is something right in front of us, and we're just not seeing it yet. How do children disappear in front of everyone's eyes? Let's think outside the box for a moment. These are young children, but not infants. They are all about the same age, and they come from families that teach them to always be aware of strangers, especially strangers in cars. So, who would these children feel comfortable going with? What would catch their curiosity enough for them to approach, without fear? I would say, in most communities, that would be an officer or a police car but, I can assure you, that would not be true in these neighborhoods."

The group, listening to Brian, laughed knowing just how true the words were.

"So, what's left? Let's hear from you. Anyone have any thoughts? Let's hear them."

One of the officers, sitting on the edge of a table, jumps in and says, "Based on what you just said, I was thinking that a kid doesn't go near anything strange; certainly not a car or person they don't know. However, they wouldn't be afraid of a vehicle that they saw on a regular basis. So, I began listing the kinds of vehicles that would travel through these neighborhoods all the time."

He takes out a small notebook, from his back pocket,

turns to a page, and begins to read the list, "Mail or garbage trucks, UPS or FedEx trucks and, sometimes, taxis. Then, there are ambulances or fire trucks. And, I'm sure there are others I haven't thought of, that would possibly entice a youngster to approach them."

He closed his notebook, and looked up at Brian.

"Good thinking Dan, let's all follow up on that. We should be able to get the schedules of most of these company's trucks, and see if they correspond to the times these children disappeared. I'll also pass the word along to the families in the neighborhood, so they can help keep an eye out for trucks that aren't supposed to stop there, like moving trucks. Anything else anyone thinking about? Remember, let's think outside the box on this case."

Just as they are discussing the various truck options, a police car rolls up to a Good Humor truck. The officer asks his partner what flavor he wants, and gets out of the car.

There are several people in front of him, so he waits until each of the adults, and their children, completes their order. One little boy holds out a handful of change to the Good Humor man, who counts the money, and hands him an ice cream cone.

Once all the other people have left, the officer approaches the truck, and says, "Business seems to be good today."

The Good Humor man responds, "Yes, the magic of this truck is amazing. All I have to do is ring my bell, as I enter a neighborhood, and they come running. I just wish I was the only one in the neighborhood. I could make a lot more money."

Curious the officer asks, "How many of you fellas are in this neighborhood?"

"According to the corporate office, there's only supposed to be two of us, but the parents keep telling me that another ice cream truck comes through the neighborhood now. It doesn't seem he's part of the Good Humor company, and he's cutting me out of money that used to be mine."

"I'll tell you what," says the officer. "If we see him around, we'll ask if he has a license to work this neighborhood. He could just be some guy trying to poach on your territory."

"Hey, that would be great, thanks. Now, what kind of cone do you want? It's on the house."

"I insist on paying. I don't want you to lose more money than you have already. I'll have two rocky roads."

The officer goes back to his car and asks his partner, "Have you noticed a Good Humor-type truck in the neighborhood, that doesn't have the Good Humor sign on it?"

"I don't think so, why?"

"Well, this fella told me his business is down because some no-name ice cream truck is selling in this neighborhood, and he's losing customers. Let's keep an eye open."

CHAPTER 33

Tom Santos, Jeff's warehouse manager, calls three of the families he distributes to, and gets the same answer. The cops are all over the neighborhood, and no one is coming down there to get their drugs when they see police cruisers all over the place. Tom then reiterates what Jeff said about either getting the drugs, and paying for them, or Jeff would cut them off and then they'd have no supply at all. He explains that another shipment is due in, and the current merchandise needs to move, and quickly. If you don't buy it, Jeff will find another place to sell it. There are always people who want the drugs he has.

After hearing his demands, Manuel decides to call the other leaders he recently met with, concerning the missing children. He had been selling drugs almost his entire life and his family, and entire neighborhood, depends on him to continue to be successful. He calls the leaders and says they need to meet again and, if there are any other leaders they know of that Jeff is supplying, have them come along.

This is a problem that needs resolution now. If they wait, and Jeff decides to sell to other people, they'd all be out of business, and that was not acceptable. That night, on the same lot where they all met before, the three young leaders, as well as two additional gang leaders meet. This was the first time that Manuel or any of the other leaders could remember that this kind of collaboration has taken place.

They are used to fighting each other for territory, but this crisis has all of them concerned. They all understand how critical the situation is, and they need to find a solution.

Manuel, who called the meeting, speaks to the group, "Jeff has us by the balls and he's squeezing. I don't fucking like being placed in this spot. Between the cops all over my neighborhood, and the missing kids, this crap has got everyone on edge. I want to know if the rest of you feel the same."

They all nodded in agreement that the problem of being cut off from their supplier was critical. Manuel asked if any of them knew of another supplier they could use, and no one did. Most of their families have been using Jeff for as long as they could remember.

Rick says, "It's time for a change. We need to take this into our own hands, and cut that motherfucker out right now."

"How?" asked one of the other leaders.

Ricky looked around and said, "We know where the warehouse is, why don't we just go over there, take the supplies, divide it up between us, and get rid of Jeff."

"Bad idea," says Manuel. "I thought of that, but what

then? Jeff's the man with the contacts. Where the fuck does he get the drugs from?"

Pat jumps in and says, "I say we go over there and grab his ass and make him tell us what we need to know. Fuck, you put a little fire under his balls, and he'll tell you anything you want."

Ricky says, "I'm okay with that, but he's got something like a dozen guys down there, and they carry, big time. You could be starting a fucking war. Where does the asshole live, maybe we can catch him there?"

No one seemed to know where he lives, so Ricky says, "We should place a number of our guys around the area of the warehouse, and follow him. If we find out where he lives, we could hit him there."

Everyone agreed.

Manuel says, "Supposing we find out all this information, then what? Who's going to approach the cartel and tell them we took over? Who wants to place their balls on the line?"

Pat says, "Nobody will be placing their balls on the line if we tell the cartel that all of us are together on this. They must already know that between us, we control the fucking distribution of drugs in this city, not that asshole Jeff. They understand money, and we will be controlling the money in this town, and they know it. First, we need to corner Jeff, and get the information we need. How about each of us send two cars down to the wharf area and surround the warehouse, so that whenever he leaves, we'll be able to follow. We just need to tell whoever you send to keep the fuck out of sight, and not get too close, or he'll panic, then we're fucked. In the meantime, we need to get some of his supply to each of us. That way we'll have some time for the change. Just have your kids do the pickups quietly, and in small quantities." They all agree, and decide to begin in the morning.

CHAPTER 34

Ed Teller woke up around 1:30 in the afternoon. His body didn't want to get out of bed, but he forced himself to get up and into the shower. When he looked in the mirror to shave, he hardly recognized the reflection. The Ed Teller he knew was gone. These two years had an awful effect on him. His eyes and face were hollow, his hair had turned totally gray, and his body reminded him of an eighty-year-old. His skin sagged, and his hands were skin and bone. He finished shaving, dressed in his white uniform, that now was a size too large, and went downstairs and made coffee. He was going to make a breakfast of eggs, but instead had a piece of toast. He drove down to Lake Drive, and pulled up next to the garage. After opening the door, and pulling the truck out, he pulled his Mercedes into the garage, closing and locking it. He climbed into the truck and headed for the ice cream factory, to pick up his daily load. Since he sold so little, at the end of each day, he disposed of the ice cream in a dumpster, near the wharf.

He knew the route he would be taking today, which changed each day, so no one would be suspicious. But, at the same time, he wanted to drive down the streets where he knew that children played outside their houses. He was driving down a quiet street when a police car came up behind him, with lights flashing. His heart began to beat so hard, he could hear it. He pulled over, and waited. If this was the end, he was completely satisfied with what he had already accomplished. He sat there as the officer approached the front door of his truck. He rolled the front window down and asked. "Is everything okay, officer? I surely wasn't speeding," he said, smiling at the officer.

"No sir. I haven't seen your truck here before. At first I thought you were a Good Humor truck, but I see it's your own rig. Can I see your permit to drive through this neighborhood?"

"Of course," Ed says, and opens his glove compartment to get the paperwork from the city. "Is there a problem with my being here?" he asks, as he hands the permit to the officer.

"No sir," answered the officer, "It's just that a number of children have disappeared in the neighborhood, and we're being extra cautious."

"Oh my," says Ed, "I'm sorry to hear that."

The officer hands back the paperwork and says, "Everything seems to be in order, sir. Can I ask you why you chose this area for your territory? While you are free to sell anywhere in the city, this is a poor, and often dangerous, neighborhood. Why here?"

"If you looked closely at my permit, you saw that I live out in Stevenson, MD. My wife and child have never had to worry about having an ice cream cone when it gets hot. These kids do. So, when I retired, I decided this is what I wanted to do. It gives me more joy than it does the kids, believe me."

The officer smiles and says, "Well, good for you. I'm sure the kids appreciate it. By the way, do you carry Rocky Road?"

"Of course, would you like one?

"Not now, but when I see you around the neighborhood, I'll know where to stop."

After the police car takes off, Ed continues down the street, turns the corner, and stops the truck. He catches his breathe, and waits until his heart rate slows down, then resumes pursuit of his next victim.

CHAPTER 35

Sitting in the Control Center, Brian is looking at the list of trucks that go in and out of the neighborhoods they are checking. There are hundreds; from delivery trucks to pickup trucks to workmen's trucks, to painters, to regular citizens going to and from their homes. He realizes just how large this problem has become. The thing that keeps unsettling him is that nothing on the list stands out as, "Wow, this is the one." His staff is working on cross-checking each of the trucks, and trucking companies, to see if their trucks were in the neighborhood on the three or four days that children disappeared. His fear is that this could take weeks, if not months, and these families aren't going to wait that long. They want answers now. Just this afternoon, his Captain called and asked him when he would see some results. The press has begun to ask what the police are doing about the missing children, as if the police were just sitting on their hands doing nothing. It was late in the day and he was awaiting reports from the various cruisers out on their respective beats.

As he sits there, pondering what to do next, a couple of officers walk into the center. One is carrying a six pack of soda. He walks over to Brian and asks, "How about a cold drink, Lieutenant?"

Brian takes one and says, "Thanks. Anything new out there?"

"Nothing but ice cream trucks," answers the police officer.

"Ice cream trucks?" questions Murphy.

"Right, we ran into a big conflict between two ice cream trucks. One a Good Humor truck and the other an independent. It seems the Good Humor guy was put out that this no-name truck was taking business away from him."

"Did the independent guy have a permit?"

"He did. He told me an interesting story."

"What kind of story?"

"When I asked him why a guy like him was selling ice cream down in the that particular neighborhood, he said his wife and son never had to worry about having ice cream in hot weather, whereas these kids did. So when he retired, he decided this is what he wanted to do. A different angle, huh?"

Brian says, "Yes, I guess so. What neighborhood was he driving through?"

"Right off Broadway, near the old Apex theater."

"Just make sure those two competitors don't get into an

altercation. That's all we need is an ice cream war," says Brian.

Ed is just about to head back to Lake Drive. It's 5 p.m. He has driven the streets all afternoon, and sold ice cream, but hasn't had the opportunity to catch a child alone. He is stacking some of the empty cartons along the wall when a knock comes on the back door. He opens the door to find two 6 or 7 year-old children standing there.

"Can we get an ice cream cone?" one asks, as he shows Ed the money in his hand.

At first Ed is about to say no but, instead, tired and frustrated, he looks at the two of them and decides on the spot, "Sure, come in and pick your flavor."

The two children climb into his truck. As they do, Ed closes the door and locks it.

He then turns to the children. "How about playing a game first?"

"What kind of game?" the young girl asks.

"It's like hide and seek. You close your eyes and I pick an ice cream flavor and if you guess the flavor, I give you the ice cream free."

Both quickly say yes, and close their eyes.

"Now, no looking," instructs Ed, as he goes into one of the drawers, and pulls out two drugged chocolate ice cream cups, and two plastic bags.

He hands the ice cream to the children, who quickly taste it, guess 'chocolate,' and then finish the ice cream. Both fall over quickly, from the drugged ice cream.

Ed quickly pulls the two plastic bags over their heads, and tightens them around the children's throats.

He waits until the two children stop breathing, and then drags them over to the false bottom of the truck. He opens it, and drops their bodies down into the opening, and then shuts and locks it. He then gets into the driver's seat, and heads to the wharf, to dump the rest of the ice cream. He thinks how happy Sharon would be right now if she knew just how well his revenge was working.

CHAPTER 36

It's late. Manuel is sitting in the basement of his home, which serves as his office.

He, and three members of his family, are counting cash receipts from the day. They are banding the cash, and dropping it into the floor safe, as they do every night.

Manuel's cell phone rings, and he quickly picks it up.

"Manuel, Murphy."

"Jesus, it's almost midnight. What's happening? Did you find the kids?"

"Unfortunately, no, not yet, but we think we have a clue. It seems that vehicles go through the Baltimore area every day, and some on a regular basis, like mail trucks. We are cross-referencing the routes, with the various truck lines, to see which trucks were in your area when your child disappeared. I'm calling to suggest to your family, and to the other families, that they keep an eye open for any truck that looks suspicious. If they see one, have them call it in right away, and we'll have a cruiser out there to check on it. Okay?"

"The message will go out now. If we find the guy that took my kid, your cruisers might not get here in time. Because if he hurt my kid, he's dead already."

"Manuel, I appreciate your anger but, remember, your family needs you more than the prison system. You identify the bastard, and let us take care of the rest."

Brian's other phone rings, and he says, "Hold on a second, my other phone is ringing." He puts the phone down and picks up his other cell phone. "Lt. Murphy," he says.

"This the place to tell about missing kids?"

"Yes, it is, why, what happened?"

The voice on the other end of the line sounded angry and terrified. Brian hears yelling in the background. "This is Jack Hubbard. My two kids are missing. They just left, about a half an hour ago, and were supposed to return home right away. They're just 6 and 7 years old. They were down along Broadway, near the old Apex theater. We've called all their friends in the neighborhood. No one has seen them. They're just two little kids. You've got to find them right away."

"Jack, what's your address? I'll have a car down there right away to begin to look for them."

Jack gave Brian his address, and then hung up.

Brian picked up the other phone, "Manuel, did you hear that?"

"I heard, man, this shit is getting out of control. What the fuck is going on? We got to stop this son of a bitch."

"You won't get an argument from me. Make sure you spread the word about the trucks, and I will follow up with Jack Hubbard to see if anyone had seen any strange trucks this evening, in his neighborhood. I'll keep you informed."

Brian dispatched two patrol cars to the Broadway area, and decided to take a ride to Jack's house, to show that the police department are concerned. He'd had a short nap, late in the afternoon, but having been up with the birth of his granddaughter, and this on-going disaster downtown, he is both tired and wired, from all the coffee he had consumed. He is about to call Sally but realizes, she too, was probably exhausted, and in bed by now, so he puts on his jacket and heads out to his police car.

CHAPTER 37

Terry laid in bed next to Monica. Their lovemaking always put her to sleep, and did the opposite for him. He was wide awake. He and Monica had spent the evening discussing the project that Brian's son-in-law was involved with. Monica's enthusiasm delighted Terry, who knew very little about real estate development. She confirmed that the area Scott and his partners were interested in, had interested her as well, but she was too busy to do anything about it. She also felt that the project was just too small. She took out some of her Baltimore maps, and showed Terry the blighted area that she had originally thought about, and he quickly understood how large it was.

"These four guys could never afford to develop this whole neighborhood. It would take a huge loan to just buy up all the properties, and level the buildings," says Terry.

"Well, now that's what our company can help with. As Dad mentioned, we do business in the bank they are working with. If we can meet with the four of them, and work out an agreement that satisfies all the parties, we could pre-empt other developers from coming into the area, and could develop all of it ourselves. It would be a big commitment for them. We could front the money but, they would have to understand that they would become minority owners in the new company we would form. However, it would end up much better for them in the long run. They could end up the premier developers in Baltimore."

"I'm sure I could manage to have the four of them meet with us. Now, that sounds odd to say 'us', rather than 'you'. I'll just have to get used to it."

She puts her arm around his shoulder, and says, "It's always been us, now it's official."

He kisses her cheek and says, "I'll try to get them to meet with us in the next few days. I'll ask them to hold off on any work they're doing, until we meet. I don't want to muddy the water. This should excite all of them but, who knows. Worst case scenario is that they end up with just the four properties."

"I think we can persuade them that this idea of theirs is wonderful. All we want to do is expand the idea, and include them in the expansion. It really is a win/win."

The next morning, Scott is on a conference call with Ralph and Tony, while Andrew sits next to him in their office. Earlier, Scott had a call from Terry, who spelled out the proposition that he and his company were willing to undertake, if the four of them were amenable. It was over-whelming, just thinking about the size and scope of the project, but he told Terry he would call his partners, and get their reaction before he met with Monica and Terry.

"We're talking about a large area. The idea is to expand the original idea, that Ralph conceptualized, and essentially do the same thing. Terry said the financing could be covered by the bank we're presently working with. They, of course, would create a new corporation, with the four of us as minority stockholders. Thinking about the scale of this project, Terry says it would make all of us rich, and probably famous. After this project is completed, we could probably name any area of Baltimore to redevelop, and get the city to back our idea."

"Sounds great," says Ralph, "But, this is no two-year commitment. This is big. Tony, are you ready to make that kind of commitment? What's going to happen to the rest of your business? This is a full-time job. And Scott, you and Andrew have been expanding your business, so you will need to be hands on as well. Maybe you won't be using a hammer, but managing the administration of this project with Terry and Monica. There are decisions that will require our attention from the get-go, the least of which is getting all the required permits and zoning handled. Hell, I'm loaded now, so I don't know just how much more time I can give to this."

"Ralph," says Scott, "This was your idea to begin with. I don't think we should go ahead with it, if you're not included. It just wouldn't feel the same. We all make a good living now, and this was supposed to be our little side project to do something together. So, if you don't want in, I'm out as well."

"I didn't say I was out, just that it's really much more than I expected out of this idea. I have to sit with it."

"How about if we all meet with Monica and Terry later today, and discuss the whole thing with them. They must understand that we're not developers, and would need a great deal of help to get this off the ground."

Andrew nods in agreement, and then Tony and Ralph agree.

"Let's meet after 5 tonight," suggests Ralph.

Scott says, "I'll get back to you two when I set up the meeting."

CHAPTER 38

On the upper floor, above Terry's office, is a conference room that Monica and her father use for meetings. It is furnished with a long, beautiful, glass top table that could seat twelve easily. The room is covered with silver and green abstract wallpaper, and the chairs are covered with a green matching fabric.

At one end of the room, there is a screen that has been lowered, for the meeting that is about to take place. There are pots of coffee around the table, with china cups for the guests, no Styrofoam cups or plastic utensils are used in this room.

The four young partners sit down, after pouring themselves coffee. They are seated next to each other, so that their view is out the large windows, looking over the harbor. Terry and Monica distribute the presentation they had prepared for discussion during the meeting. As the four partners begin to review the document, a newcomer walks into the room. He looks like an undertaker, dressed in a black suit and tie, with a white shirt. He is maybe 5'6", thin, and slightly bent over. Monica quickly introduces him to the group.

"Gentlemen, this is our company's chief accountant, Michael Tourney. He has been with the firm for almost 30 years, and is considered one of the finest real estate experts in the state. I thought it would be wise to have him here to answer any questions you might have, regarding our proposal. So, let's begin. Each of you has a packet in front of you. In it are maps and research about the neighborhood we are proposing to redevelop with you. It's not complicated but, if it's okay with you, I would like to spend a few minutes going over each page. So why don't we begin with the map of the neighborhood, and the blocks we've identified for development?"

After almost an hour and a half, going through the presentation packet, and slides of the proposed area in question, Monica says, "If you don't have questions, I'd be surprised. So let's hear them."

Ralph, who was taking notes during the entire presentation, asks, "Are you saying that your company will determine the blocks we develop, pick the architect we use, and bankroll the entire project? Because if that's what I hear, then why do you need us?"

"Excellent question, Ralph," answers Monica. "I'm sure all of you feel the same, at least I would, if I were in your shoes. Let me explain something, and I think Terry will probably jump in as well. You might not know that my father's company owns a large number of buildings in and around Baltimore. He buys them, and sometimes sells them but, most of the time, he leases out space to companies and individuals. We, my father and I, have never been in the development business. Whereas you four have created this wonderful concept for condos, just north of downtown Baltimore. When Terry told me and my father about it, both of us agreed that we wanted nothing to do with the day-to-day development of these condos. However, what we would like is to expand on your idea, and develop the entire neighborhood, but with the four of you taking the lead. You guys determine which architect we use, how many condos per unit, the size of each unit, etc. You would have our full cooperation in facilitating financing, and any additional expertise we can offer. Michael can show you shortcuts to getting things accomplished in the city, and be your expert on what to spend, how to spend it, and how to make the most profit per unit. He has been our expeditor for years, and now he can be yours. He will help you do this without lowering your standards for the buildings. The four of you will be the management of this new company. We will insist that Michael be made a corporate officer, looking after not only your best interests, but mine and my father's as well. This project could end up costing somewhere between 80 and 100 million dollars. The profit we hope will be at least that much. With my company owning 70 percent of the stock, and the four of you 30 percent. The simple math of this is that each of you have the potential of making between 8 and 10 million dollars, based on our preliminary costs of acquisition and construction. I can assure you the cost of these condos will go up after the first units have been sold, so the numbers I just gave you are conservative. Your decision is sort of obvious. Do you want to build only the four properties you currently own, or can you see the big picture? This is not a sales pitch. Terry will tell you that I am a salesperson, so it's hard for me not to sell. But if you decide not to pursue this proposal, I will not hold it against you in the least."

Terry says, "Listen, this is a lot to take in. We don't need decisions today, but we want the four of you, who are business people in your own right, to go home and think about this. You might also consider something that Monica and I discussed last night, while putting this proposal together. How about using inner city youth to do the hard labor, and train them on the job? That way they have opportunities to become carpenters and plumbers and other good paying trades? Also, in the future, if this whole project is successful, we will have a resident supply of skilled workers. However, right now this is all pie in the sky. That is, until the four of you give us the go ahead to create this company, and begin redeveloping the neighborhood. Remember, this was your idea. We're only here for support."

"By the way, we want to keep the name of the corporation 4 Baltimore, it's wonderful." Monica says, "Any other questions?"

There is silence as the four look back and forth at each other. Scott says, "Thank you for the presentation. It was amazing. However, if I don't get some sleep soon, I'm going to drop. I want to see my wife and baby girl before I col-lapse."

Both Monica and Terry say simultaneously, "mazel tov!"

The four guests leave the building and, as they walk down the block to their cars, Tony says, "Jesus, that presen-tation was amazing. It was overwhelming. Do you believe we can pull this off?"

Ralph says, "Look, let's take Terry's advice, and sleep on it. You're right, the project they're talking about is much bigger than we had originally planned, but that doesn't mean it's impossible to accomplish. Right now, I'm wiped out, and I'm going home. I'll talk to you tomorrow." The four split up and take off.

CHAPTER 39

On Lake Drive, Ed has been in the basement most of the night with the bodies of the children. He's half sleeping from exhaustion and giggling. "Six little bodies lying on the ground, six little bodies will never be found."

Over and over he repeats the short poem, and giggles. His head falls onto his chest, his eyes close, and tears begin to pour down his cheeks and onto the front of his white shirt. He lifts his head and thinks, it was so close today, so close. That officer had me. All he had to do was ask if I was the one who took the children, and I would have spit out the whole story.

Where are the police? Maybe they don't care about the inner city kids disappearing. Maybe that's what they want. Less kids growing up to shoot each other, and innocent children. Wouldn't that be wonderful? It's too late, too late, too late. His eyes close as his head drops to his chest again but, this time, he falls asleep.

Later, he awakens, sits up, and almost tips over the chair.

His eyes are trying to focus. He looks at his watch to see what time it is. It says 4:00 but, because the windows are all blacked out, he doesn't know if that's morning or night. He goes up the stairs of the basement, cracks the door, and sees that it's still light out, so he knows that it's late afternoon. He realizes he's been asleep for almost six hours, the most he's slept in days. Yet, he doesn't feel refreshed, he feels more tired than he can remember. He's beginning to smell the dead bodies for the first time, even though the basement is very cool, and the bodies are completely wrapped in heavy plastic. He thinks that it's already too late to get home, shower, change into a clean uniform, and then make it back to the next neighborhood.

Probably the best thing to do is take the rest of today off. He goes outside, gets into his car, and heads back to Stevenson. Arriving there he retrieves the mail from the mailbox, and takes it into the house. He drops the mail onto the kitchen table, and goes upstairs to take a shower. However, realizes how hungry he is and, instead, goes back downstairs, washes his face and hands in the kitchen, and looks in the refrigerator to see what he has to eat. It's empty except for some 1% milk, which he opens, to smell if it's still good. It isn't. "Shit," he says, "I need to get something to eat."

Rather than go out in his dirty uniform, he goes back upstairs, showers, and puts on khakis and a polo shirt, and heads out to a restaurant. He drives down to Pikesville where he knows of several places that he and Sharon had frequented. He arrives at his favorite seafood restaurant and walks in. It's early, and they are just setting up for their dinner crowd. When the owner sees Ed, he comes over and greets him, "Hello, I haven't seen you here in a while. Where's your lovely wife? Sharon, isn't it?"

"She's feeling under the weather, so rather than have her cook, I thought I'd come down here and bring a couple crab cakes home to her. You think you could put that together for me?"

"Why of course, can I get you a glass of wine while you're waiting?"

"Yes, thanks, Chardonnay."

Twenty-five minutes later, Ed is on his way home with 2 orders of crab cakes, and the rest of the bottle of Chardonnay sitting next to him. He's feeling light-headed from the two glasses of wine he drank while waiting, and almost hits a pedestrian walking across the street, near Slade and Reisterstown Road. He doesn't look back, since he missed the woman but, within a minute, a police car comes up behind him, flashing his lights.

"Oh, for Christ sake," thinks Ed. "What now?"

The officer slowly gets out of his car and approaches Ed's Mercedes. When he almost reaches the front door, Ed opens his driver's side window and asks, "Is everything okay, sir?"

The officer approaches the open window, smells alcohol on Ed's breath, and notices the open bottle next to him. He backs off a step and, with a commanding voice, says "Please get out of the car."

"What's the problem?" Ed asks, beginning to sweat.

"Just get out of the car, sir. You almost hit a pedestrian at

Slade Avenue and, from what I can tell, you've had a bit too much to drink."

Speaking a little louder the officer commands, "Get out of the car!"

Ed unbuckles his seat belt, and opens the door. He slowly gets out of the car, and almost stumbles. The officer says "Please lean against the car, sir."

Ed begins to say something, but thinks better of it. The officer takes out a gauge and asks Ed to blow into it. Ed again begins to ask, what for, but hesitates, and allows the officer place the gauge in his mouth. He blows into it and feels woozy.

The officer says, after reading the gauge, "You better come with me, sir."

He takes Ed's arm, leads him to the police car, cuffs him, and carefully places him in the back seat. He then gets on the police radio and calls in to his station. "I have a DUI, just west of Slade, on Reisterstown. He's pulled over, out of traffic, so I'll lock his car and bring the keys in with me."

"10-4," comes the response.

The officer says to Ed, "Your alcohol level is almost double the legal limit. Can I see your driver's license?"

Ed struggled to get his wallet out of his back pocket, finds his license, and hands it to the officer.

"Edward Teller. It says here your address is in Stevenson, is that still correct?"

"Yes," answers Ed, now getting a little angry over the whole business, and trying his best to hold onto his temper. He keeps thinking, these are the same cops that could not find the person who shot my son, because they were hiding out catching people who had a little too much to drink.

"Is the registration in your car?"

"In the glove compartment," answers Ed.

After the officer assures himself that Ed is the owner of the car, he takes the registration and license with him, gets into the police car, and looks back at Ed.

"We're heading to the station. Hopefully, a night in custody will remind you that drinking and driving is dangerous."

Ed leans back and tries to stay awake. He realizes he's still hungry, and the crab cakes are sitting on the back seat of his car.

CHAPTER 40

Manuel calls Jack Hubbard and asks, "Your kid missing?"

"Both my little ones are missing. My wife is going crazy. I tell her that other kids are missing too, but she don't give a shit about other kids, just her two babies."

"Mine too," says Manuel. "You tell her we going to get the fucker who's doing this. I guarantee it, okay."

"Yeah, okay, but do it soon."

As he finishes talking to Manuel, one of his kids runs in and says, "Some cop's at the door. Says he talked to you already on the phone."

"Bring him back here."

Brian walks in, and introduces himself. Then asks Jack if anyone has seen the children, or heard from them.

"Nothing. They ran out together to get ice cream, and that's the last anyone has seen them."

"Ice cream?" Brian says.

"Yeah. The Good Humor truck drops by, and the kids get a cone."

"You sure it was a Good Humor truck?"

"Yeah, I guess. Who else is selling ice cream in this neighborhood?"

Not wanting to panic Jack, Brian says, "You're right. I'll get in touch with the Good Humor people, and see if one of their drivers saw your children last night. If he did, that would help a lot. Thanks."

"In addition, there are two patrol cars circling this neighborhood. If your children reappear, they'll be brought right home. If you hear of anything, please call me, and we'll move right on it."

Back in his car, Brian calls the Operation Center and tells them to get ahold of the two officers that saw that rogue ice cream truck, and have them call him right away. He told them he would be headed over to the Center, and that he wanted all his staff there for a meeting in an hour. After so many disappointing clues in the case, Brian felt this might be the one break that they needed. If that ice cream vendor was their man, Brian thought, then he's getting sloppy. Picking up two kids, when the parents knew they were going out for ice cream, was his first mistake. Now, let's see if we can locate him before he does more damage. The question is, where is he keeping the children? Does he have them locked away somewhere? And, why is he taking these kids? Once they locate the truck, they need to be very careful, and not spook the guy until they know where he's holding the kids.

Brian is standing in front of a dozen officers; all have been working overtime. They've been looking through the neighborhoods for strange trucks and cars; plus, doing their routine duties taking care of domestic arguments, petty thefts, home break-ins, and the like. They all look like they could use two weeks in Hawaii.

Brian understands this, since he too has been running on tomorrow's energy , especially with the time he has spent with his daughter at the hospital. He starts off with a smile, "So, I think we have a big break in this case. It seems there is a rogue ice cream truck operating in the neighborhood where the two children disappeared last night. By chance, two officers saw and spoke to him last night. According to their investigation, the regular Good Humor truck driver was angry because this guy was working in his territory. I'm waiting for the officers to get back to me with this driver's name and description. In the meantime, what I need to know – and it will take some house-to-house canvassing – is whether this truck was seen in the last week around the other neighborhoods where children are missing? Let's find this guy. But if you find him, be cautious, we want him alive and talking about where he's keeping the missing children. That is our primary focus right now. Although I promised I would keep the families informed, giving them this information could cause more problems if they find him before we do. They might string him up on the nearest lamppost. So, let's keep our suspicions, regarding this rogue ice cream truck, under your hats for the time being. This is a big break, let's take advantage of it."

Brian then drives over to the station and checks in. The place seems quiet, except for an officer checking in some old fella he brought in on a DUI, who looked like two days sleep wouldn't hurt him. Brian walked past them to his office, as the Captain called out to him. "Hey Brian, you have a second?"

"Sure," as he headed for the Captain's office.

Captain Kessler had been Brian's boss and friend for thirty years. Kessler was a sergeant when Brian joined the force, and had encouraged him to continue his education. He was not a big person, around 5'10", but built solid. His most distinctive feature was his bald head, which he kept clean and shined like a bowling ball. Most of the officers, at one time or another, had begun to call him "Strike" because of it. He didn't mind, as long as they did their jobs, he let them have all the fun they wanted. He knew from his thirty-five years as a cop in Baltimore, he needed a healthy sense of humor to get him through each day.

Brian entered the Captain's office and sat down across from him, letting out an old man's sigh. The Captain laughed and said, "So Grandpa, congratulations. Bridget and the baby doing okay?"

"Everyone's fine but Sally and me. I think we were less tired when Bridget was born. I'm not sure if having grandchildren is going to be a blessing or not. Right now, I'm too tired to know."

"Believe me, Brian, it just gets better every day. Once the child is old enough to take to the zoo, you'll understand how wonderful it is. So, tell me what's happening with the case of the disappearing children?"

"I think we caught a break." Brian briefs him about his conversation with Jack Hubbard, and the information from an officer, describing the turf conflict between the two ice cream trucks.

"Brian, it's not a break, it's how your mind works. It's your ability to see how the puzzle pieces fit together. Give yourself a pat on the back, and let's catch this bastard."

Brian gets up and heads over to his office. He calls Sally, and gets an update on Bridget.

"Scott is picking us up in a little while. He called from home and said he was on the way. Bridget looks wonderful, but feeling a little sore right now. She'll be fine after a couple days in bed. The baby, what can I say, gorgeous. She has Scott's blue eyes, but looks just like her mom."

"Actually, I thought she looked just like you," says Brian. "That's why she's so pretty."

"Alright you old man, leave me alone. When are you coming home?"

"I hope to get there for dinner. Are you going to be at home, or at Scott's?"

"I don't know. Call me later and I'll tell you, okay."

"Okay but, promise me, you'll stop at home long enough to take a nap. You're not as young as you used to be. Maybe you can nap at Scott's."

"I'm a lot younger than you. So take your own advice and try to get some shut eye. I know you, Mr. Murphy."

"I'll try. I'll talk to you later, sweetheart."

As he hung up, his phone rang. "Murphy."

"Lt., this is Sergeant Acosta. I think your information might be paying off. Two different neighborhoods have acknowledged seeing and buying from the rogue ice cream truck. I've cautioned all the stations to be on a lookout for the guy. I've also briefed them on how important it is that we capture him alive, so we can find out where he's holding the children. This was the break we were looking for."

"Thanks, sergeant. I appreciate the update. Just keep me posted."

CHAPTER 41

———— ✺ ————

Jack Hubbard is sitting in his living room with his two brothers and several other members of their family. "My kids went out for ice cream from a Good Humor truck and never came home. I'm not waiting for the cops to find my kids. They couldn't find their asses with both hands. Tomorrow, start looking for that Good Humor ice cream truck, bring the son of a bitch here, and let's hear what he has to say. If he took my kids, I'm going to cut his balls off and feed them to him. Be careful, the whole area is covered with police cruisers. You all have your cells, so call me when you spot him. If you can't bring him here, I'll come out to where he is and have a heart-to-heart talk. Find out from the kids what time he usually hits our neighborhood. It should be tomorrow afternoon sometime. Let's play this cool."

An hour later, sitting side-by-side in a blue Chevy, Jack's two younger brothers talk about their missing nephew and niece. Juan, in the driver's seat, is 17 years old. He has been part of his brother's gang since he was old enough to remember. He has a mean looking scar across his forehead from a fight he instigated. He is still growing and was now almost as tall as Jack, whom he worshipped. He knew everything Jack was involved with, from pills to cocaine, and had started out on the street corner selling them. , he supervised other younger kids operating in a six block area.

His younger brother Mateo, seated next to him, was his right-hand man, and followed him around like a puppy dog. He was not the smartest child in the family but, at 14, he could handle himself physically. He had proven himself several years ago, in a gun fight downtown, when he killed a rival gang member who ventured into their territory by mistake. Unfortunately, some kid was shot and died during the gun fight. That was two years ago. Mateo still carried a gun, but no longer had the gun that killed the kid; that gun ended up in the Bay the night of the shooting.

"I think the ice cream guy starts around Holland Avenue. Why don't we get down there early, have some breakfast, and wait for him to show," says Robby.

Mateo smiles and says, "Great, we could bring him back here ourselves. Jack would like that."

Juan and Mateo have finished their McDonald's breakfasts and park along the route usually taken by the ice cream truck that goes through their neighborhood. They have been told by a number of kids that the truck leaves the Good Humor warehouse around 10 a.m. By 9:30 a.m. they are parked a few blocks from the fenced-in warehouse, making sure they don't miss him.

Both brothers have taken uppers, and are feeling anxious for the moment when the truck arrives. Both have guns. They feel like Jessie and Frank James, whom they have admired ever since they saw an old movie on TV about the outlaw brothers. Their car becomes their horses and, the ice cream truck, their train to capture. They both feel the tension and excitement build.

A few blocks away Ben Trull, a 59 year old Good Humor man who has a personality that fits his job, is filling his truck with the products he knows he will need for the day. Along with his pleasant disposition, he has a face that kids warm to. His smile is almost constant, and it is obvious he enjoys the time he spends with the children. It will be a warm day, so he knows he will be busy, even if the other ice cream truck shows up. He also knows not to put high-priced ice cream products in the truck, because most of the kids in his neighborhood usually only buy cones. He has collected his money bag, containing enough change for the day, and places it in a safe place in back of the driver's seat.

Ben's been traveling up and down these streets for 30 years. His dream was to go to college, and become a doctor, but his parent's separation, then his father taking off, meant that both he and his mother had to find work to survive. Although he was accepted at University of Maryland, he had to work. A friend told him about the need for Good Humor drivers. At first he thought he would do this job only until he saved enough to go to College Park; however, he found he liked it. He was on his own, he was with all sorts of people all day, and the joy he experienced when the kids came running to his truck was what kept him on the job. He also liked the respect he received from the parents when he went out of his way to care for their children; like yelling at the little ones when they ran across the street to his truck without looking both ways, or having them stand in line to wait their turn.

Many times one of their parents would come by for an ice cream cone, and hand him an extra couple bucks to say thanks. He made a good living, and looked forward to moving down south in five years when he retired with his wife, Mary Ann, who was an ER nurse. Both their girls lived in North Carolina, with their families, and wanted them to come down to be with their grandchildren. He felt blessed, and knew Mary Ann did as well. They've had a good life, and raised two wonderful children.

When he had finished loading up his truck, Ben went into the main office to tell everyone he was leaving, and then climbed into his truck. He had driven less than a half dozen blocks when a blue Chevy pulled in front of him at a light, and a young boy hopped out, and pointed a gun at him. He froze. The boy yelled, "Get out of the truck now or I'll blow your head off."

He reached down to turn the truck engine off and, James thinking he was going for a gun, fired through the window. The bullet hit Ben across the top of his head. Since he was bent down, his body went forward and the horn began to blast.

Mateo panicked and jumped back in the car. "Let's get out of here."

Juan accelerated, and drove away as fast as the car would

go, while yelling to his brother, "What the fuck did you do?! We were supposed to bring him back to Jack. He's going to cut you a new asshole."

Within minutes of the gun shot, a police car pulled up. The officer called in the shooting, and quickly examined Ben. His heartbeat was slow, and there was blood running down his shirt, but he was alive.

An ambulance rushed Ben to the hospital ER, where it happened that his wife Mary Ann was on duty. She heard from another nurse what had occurred and was at Ben's side immediately. He hadn't regained consciousness, but the prognosis was good, so she took the day off from her other duties and sat with him, holding his hand and checking his vitals.

Three different officers called in to Brian to tell him about the shooting. He was furious. There was no doubt that either Jack Hubbard or one of his family was responsible for the shooting. He was the only one that Brian had discussed the ice cream vendor with. He got on the phone and called Jack, trying not to sound too angry, and begin a verbal confrontation with the young man.

"Jack, this is Murphy. What's going on down there? I've had a number of reports of a shooting at a Good Humor truck. Are you still keeping quiet on this, or are we going to have to lock down your neighborhood ?"

"Shit, man, it wasn't us. What the fuck you accusing me of ?"

"I'm not accusing you of anything, right now, but a Good Humor man is in the hospital, with a gunshot wound, and City Hall wants me to clamp down on the gangs who did this. This is bad Jack, really bad. We don't even know if it was a Good Humor man that took the children, and already someone is trying to kill them. I want you to pull some strings down there, and stop this now, do you understand me? You really don't want to piss the police department off, and you sure as hell don't want to get your community against you for shooting their Good Humor men, you get me Jack?"

"I hear you, but I didn't do this."

"Personally, I don't give a shit who did it right now, I just want it to stop. You get on the phone and tell everyone that Lt. Murphy is on the warpath and, if he finds another Good Humor man with even a cut finger, he's coming down there with an army." Brian hung up and sat back in his chair. "Goddamn it all. Thank God the man was not seriously hurt, although he might not think so right now. I think I'll run down to the hospital, and see what I can find out."

CHAPTER 42

There are coincidences that occur, which no one knows about. Sometimes they have profound meanings, most of the time they're just coincidences. Later that night Brian is sitting at his desk, finishing his daily report. His eyes are not focusing the way they should, so he rubs them. He understands just how exhausted he is, but wants to finish the paperwork, about his conversation with Jack Hubbard, before he heads home. He stops writing, and figures, if he puts his head down on the desk for a minute or two, and lets his eyes rest, he'll be fine.

At the same time, Ed Teller, in a holding cell several floors below Brian, sits on a bench away from the other two drunks, one of whom has thrown up all over himself, and tries to clear his head. He knows that he should have had something to eat earlier, and that the two glasses of wine he had probably affected him because his stomach was empty. He is still hungry, but he is more tired than he could ever remember. He, too, closes his eyes and, almost immediately, sitting up, with his chin on his chest, falls asleep.

Brian wakes with a start. Almost two hours later, angry at himself, he decides not to finish the paperwork, heads out the door, and drives home. Sally is not there. She left a phone message that she was staying over at Bridget and Scott's place for the night. So, Brian takes a shower, and drops into bed at 2 a.m.

Ed won't wake up until 7 a.m., when the officer bangs on the cell and says, "Everyone up, we're going to take a ride to see the judge."

Ed awakens suddenly and sees the officer banging on the cell door. He tries to stand, but his fatigue is overwhelming, and he staggers back onto the bench.

The policeman notices and says, "Boy, you must have put one on last night."

In court, the judge fines and admonishes him after hearing his story of forgetting to eat all day, and having two glasses of wine, instead of coffee. He admits guilt, and writes a check to the city.

His car has been towed. He takes a cab to pick up his car and, again, writes a check to the city for the tow. Luckily, he has always kept a few checks in his wallet. A habit he got into when Sharon would take him to galleries "just to look."

Once in the car, he heads back to his home. All he can think about is dumping his clothes in the washing machine, and taking a long hot shower. He begins to think of the bodies at Lake Drive, and wonders if the smell would be noticeable from outside by now. The houses are not on a block frequented by many people. There would be no mailmen coming or deliveries made but, as he drove toward his home, the problem sat in the back of his mind. He began to think about the end game, and how he had planned it from the beginning. He knew that he would be caught. He knew, because he wanted it to happen. He wanted to stand in front of a jury and tell them what these killers, and the Baltimore police, had done to his family. He wanted them to judge him *after* they heard the whole story.

He especially wanted the newspapers, and other media around Baltimore, to understand how he became the monster they all had a hand in creating. Then, he wondered whose side would they come down on, the killers, or a well-respected citizen, who lost everything. He needed to find out.

When he arrived home he took out his original plan, and looked for the telephone numbers of the people that he wanted to call. He pulled out one of the burner phones he had purchased, and made sure it was charged. He did not want his calls to be traced back to him, as yet. He began with the *Baltimore Sun* newspaper. He dialed and waited for an answer. Instead, he heard the message on the answering system, "*Baltimore Sun* newspaper, if you know extension of the person you are calling, please dial it now, if not..."

Ed hit "o" and waited. A young woman answered, and asked, "This is the *Baltimore Sun*, how may I help you?"

"As a matter of fact, I think I might be able to help you, if you would put me through to your editor."

"May I ask what this is about, sir?"

"You may, but I need to speak with your editor, and I'm sure he will be very pleased that you transferred me to him."

"Please hold for a minute."

The silence only lasted for a second until the music filled the phone. After about a minute, the young lady returned to the phone and said, "Thank you for your patience. The editor is in a meeting right now. May I have your phone number and have him call you back?"

"No, you can't have my phone number but, I would suggest you call your editor back, and tell him that you have someone on the phone that has information about missing children and he could, if he gets his rear end in gear, get an exclusive."

Again, Ed is put on hold and listens to the music.

This time, when the music ends, a man's voice comes on and asks, with authority, and some anger," Who is this, and what do you know about missing children?"

"I won't tell you who this is but, I will tell you that the missing children are a direct result of the crime in this city, and the incompetence of our police department. They were kidnapped in broad daylight, from our supposedly safe Baltimore streets and, so far, our police department hasn't a clue what took place, or why. Well, I'll tell you the why, as long as you print it on the front page of your paper. The children were taken as a means of revenge. Revenge for the murder of innocent people throughout our city, who are sick and tired of these drive-by killings, without arrests. Ask yourself who causes these drive-by shootings, and check to see whose children have disappeared, and you will begin to understand what the cause and effect is." Ed hangs up.

The editor, Ralph Lesser, yells to the receptionist, "Did you get his name?"

"No sir, he wouldn't give it."

"Goddamn it! Get Bob Turner, and tell him to come to my office right away."

Within minutes, Bob, a 38 year-old crime reporter for *The Sun*, comes strolling into Ralph's office.

"What's going on, Ralph?"

"How the hell should I know? I'm always the last to know, Goddamn it. I just got off the phone with some kook, who tells me that the missing kids downtown are missing as revenge for drive-by killings. I want to know how many of these took place over the last couple years, the police investigations on them, and the results. If nothing else, we can make a front page piece out of the story."

"I'll check it out but, if you remember, there were a lot of drive-bys during the gang wars around that time. Let me do some research, and I'll get back to you."

"Keep this quiet. If it's true, that these are revenge kidnappings, we could have a big story here, and an exclusive."

After Ed hung up from *The Sun*, he called WBAL-TV and went through the same process, hanging up before they could trace his call. He then walked upstairs, showered, and went to bed.

CHAPTER 43

One of Pat's men sees the new Porsche, driven by Jeff, enter the warehouse. He writes down the license number, calls it in to Pat, who then calls a friend of his who does computer work, and tells him he needs to locate the address of the owner of the car. When asked why, he tells him the fucker just left a scratch on his BMW and left the scene but, one of the boys caught his license, and he's going to surprise him when he gets home.

Ten minutes later he has the address, on the eastern shore, and immediately calls the other families to tell them he's going over there and case the place. If any of them want to join in the fun, he gives them the address. Manuel reminds him that the object is to get the information before we kill the fucker.

They figure they could all be in place by noon, so they set up to meet a couple blocks from the home and to check it out. There are five of them. They split up, and circle the block in their cars, looking at the home from every angle.

Afterward, they return and meet together down the street. They all noticed that in front of the garage is an old Honda. Ricky says, "Someone's home. I'm going to ring the bell and ask if the owner wants to buy solar for his house. I'll get a look at the inside, and come back here. Otherwise, I'll call."

After several minutes, Ricky calls and tells them to quietly walk over to the home and come in. They go one at a time, and enter the home, so as not to arouse suspicion. Ricky is sitting in the living room with a gun pointed at an elderly Hispanic lady, who has been crying. Manuel walks over to her and begins to speak in Spanish to her. He asks her when Jeff was due home. She tells him that he is due around 3 p.m. and then he's going out for the evening, to a card game.

Manuel translates this to the others and they all smile. She then says, "I need to leave, Mr. Jeff doesn't want me here when he returns." Instead, Manuel asks her for her car keys. She fumbles through her purse, hands him a ring of keys, and shows him the one to her car.

Manuel says to the others, "I'm going to move her car down the street, and I'll be back. I don't want Jeff to see it when he comes home. In the meantime, see if the fucker has anything to eat. It's lunchtime."

CHAPTER 44

Ralph is sitting across from his father, in his downtown law firm. His father, a short, good looking man who has worn a trimmed mustache since he left law school, listened to his son tell him about the proposal that Monica and Terry presented to the four of them. There was no doubt about what Leonard Shapiro felt about his son. There was more than just father-son admiration. He had watched his son become a successful lawyer in the Baltimore/Washington corridor, when there were lawyers tripping over each other for business. His son had earned the admiration of the entire firm based on some of the cases he had handled for them. Now what he was hearing didn't sound like an outside hobby. Rather than discourage him, he listened, and quickly realized this could be a big opportunity for the firm , and especially for Ralph. When Ralph had finished, his father asked, "Do you know who Sol Kaminsky is?"

"That's Monica's father."

"Yes, but do you know who he is?"

"He owns real estate around downtown, and I've heard rumors that he has a piece of the Orioles, but what does that have to do with the project? It's Monica who's fronting the money for this project."

"Sol Kaminsky is a powerful ally to have. Yes, he has real estate and he probably has a piece of the Orioles baseball team but, he also has interests in banks, restaurants, and God only knows what else. I know that Monica says she and Terry are backing this project but, believe me when I tell you that her father had to give his blessing first. Now, what does that mean to you? First, you now become a player in helping redevelop the inner-city, and you become partners with Sol Kaminsky. If this project is what you say it is, and I have no reason to believe that it isn't, then there is no reason in the world that the four of you won't become major developers in Maryland. This is a wonderful future for you."

"So," asks Ralph, "what do you see as the downside?"

"Actually, I don't see any, right now. What impressed me was that Monica brought her accountant in, to facilitate the creation of the company, but she did not bring in a lawyer. Terry Stein also mentioned that they want to hire a number of minority kids to educate them in the building trades. What if we set up a new department here, and hire a few minority real estate lawyers to work with you? You begin to see the picture?"

"Where are we going to find those lawyers?"

"Ralph, you know how many lawyers in Baltimore are chasing car accidents to make a living? I bet if we called the universities in and around Baltimore and Washington, we'd find a handful of really qualified young minority lawyers. This could help Monica and, at the same time, help you and the firm to grow. Our firm would also have the inside track on future work for Sol Kaminsky."

"I knew you'd find a way to make more money for the firm," Ralph says, smiling at his father. I'll call Monica and Terry and tell them about your idea. They'll love it."

"You'll probably have to back off of some of your cases. Have you thought of who in the firm you want to handle them? It's important to have the new person fully brought up to speed before you get too involved in this project."

"Sandy Robb has been my second on many of these cases, and I would feel very comfortable letting him handle them going forward. However, I understand what this project will entail. I'll help you find the new lawyers I'll need for the work the development will create."

Ralph stands up, and goes over to his father. The two hug before Ralph leaves to go to his office. He sits down and calls Monica. She doesn't answer, so he tries Terry. He knows he should call his partners, but feels he has to get Monica and Terry to approve the idea first.

Also, this has to do with his and his Dad's firm more than it has to do with the new project. He knows they'll understand. If this comes together the way Monica has outlined it, all of them would benefit.

Terry answers, "Terry Stein."

"Terry, Ralph, you have a minute?"

"Of course, what can I do for you? Have the four of you come to a decision?"

"I think the answer will be positive, but that's not why I called. I spoke to my father about the project this morning. He suggested that our firm hire a couple minority lawyers to handle the increased workload that will be generated from the project. He believes this will set an example to the other businesses in Baltimore."

"Personally, it sounds like a fine move on your part. It also keeps all the work in-house. That should save us some money in the long run. Have you spoken to Monica about this?" asks Terry.

"I tried. She didn't answer."

"That's okay, I'll talk to her later and bring her up to date."

"Thanks," Ralph says.

CHAPTER 45

Brian was at the hospital, with two officers, talking about the shooting. He had stopped in to see Mary Ann, an ER nurse and wife of the driver who was shot, and give her his assurance that he would do everything he could to find the person or persons who did this to her husband. But he knew there was little or no chance that he could do that unless someone turned in the shooter, which was unlikely. He was told by the officers what was found when they arrived at the scene. Luckily, they were only a couple blocks away when someone called in the shooting. They found skid marks and an empty shell casing just outside the truck. Their additional observations interested Brian as well.

"Whoever shot him wasn't very tall. The angle of the shot came from below the door. If it had been a full-grown person, the shot would have penetrated his skull rather than just bounce off the top of his head. That means that whomever shot him was probably some kid, from a local gang, trying to make his mark."

Brian knew that he had been correct in calling Jack Hubbard. Hopefully, he took his call to heart. This had to stop. While he was nearby, he thought he'd drive around and talk to the other families, and plea with them as well, to keep the lid on, and let the police take care of finding the person who was taking their children.

Brian's phone rings and he pulls it out of his pocket and answers, "Murphy."

"Lieutenant, officer Barry Sachs here."

"What's going on, Barry?"

"Well, I'm having lunch at that trendy new bar, Halfway House, and the TV is on, and I hear the guy say that the missing kids were taken by someone who is seeking revenge on the gangs for their drive-by shootings. You know anything about this?"

"What station was it on?"

"Let me ask, hold on."

He comes back on the line and says, "WBAL-TV."

"Thanks Barry, I'll check it out."

Brian immediately calls the station and gets ahold of the TV news show's producer.

"Lt. Murphy here. So, tell me, where did this information come from?"

"Some fella called into the station and told us he knew that the kids were taken because of drive-by shootings. We're not exactly sure which shootings, because there were so many of them during the gang war, but we have our staff working on it now. We believe this might be the reason, not that it is definitely the reason. We're following up on the story as we speak. If it's true, it would explain why it's only the gang kids that have gone missing.

Brian says, "If you hear anything about who this fellow might be, you have my number, please call me."

"You know we will, Lieutenant."

As he hangs up, he thinks to himself, ice cream vendors, mysterious callers, what the hell is going on? Revenge. It would have to be some indescribable act of violence to have someone resort to this level of revenge. It would have had to be a case here in Baltimore, and probably committed during one of the gang shootings. Where in the hell do you start looking for a needle in a haystack. He picked up his phone, called his sergeants, and told them to meet him right away.

When they were all together, Brian asked them if they had heard the rumor that the missing kids were kidnapped because of some kind of revenge. They had all heard one version or another.

Brian says, "Can any of you remember a drive-by shooting in the city that was so high-profile that it showed up in the papers or on TV? Something within the last five years?"

"Shit, Lieutenant, we've had a boatload of drive-by shootings over that time, especially between the gangs. However, they wouldn't kidnap kids, they'd just come back and kill someone from the other gang."

"I agree," says Brian, "So we're talking about someone getting killed by a shooter, outside the gang, and we know that happens too often. Hell, we had one last week where a kid was killed in his house, in his crib, when a bullet went through the wall from a drive-by. So, this is what we know.

The kidnapper is not a gang member; he is a civilian. He is pissed off enough to go after the children of gang members, and he has more balls than brains, because if the gangs catch him, they'll skin him alive."

One of the sergeants says, "The person or persons would have to have access to the areas where these kids are. I mean every eye on the street would be on a stranger."

Another sergeant says, "They would have to have wheels and a place to hide the kids until they were out of the neighborhood. And they would have to do this without drawing attention to themselves."

Brian says, "Revenge is an obsession. Someone has to go over the edge to get to that point, especially with children."

Brian picks up his phone and calls Terry.

"Terry, I'm glad I caught you. Have you heard the latest WBAL report regarding the kidnappings?"

"Yes, it seems logical that someone would seek revenge on the people who caused him the pain of having a loved one murdered."

"But children, why would someone go after children?"

"Offhand, I would say that the person is seeking revenge because they lost a child during one of these drive-by shootings."

"So, we're looking for someone who lost a child in the last five years, in Baltimore, who is not a gang member, and has access to the neighborhoods. Thanks, Terry. I'll get back to you."

Brian hangs up, looks over at his staff, and says, "Gentlemen, we have to start digging into our case files, and find this person. He or she is out there waiting to be caught, otherwise why would they be calling the TV station? We need to close this out as quickly as possible. If you need more hands, get them, use overtime. Whatever it takes, I want this person behind bars."

CHAPTER 46

In the meantime, at The Sun, Ralph Lesser is livid as he yells at Bob Turner. "WBAL just announced that they think revenge was the reason for the children being kidnapped. They could not have gotten that from anyone other than that asshole who called me. He played us. We need to get on top of this story now. Get someone to help you go through the archives, and check on these drive-by shootings, and let's see if we can uncover the bastard's name."

Bob gets up out of his chair and walks slowly to his desk, picks up the phone, and waits for the ringing to stop.

"What?" comes the answer.

"I can't make it tonight."

"Fuck you, Bob. This is the third time you've broken our date. If you don't want to get together, just tell me. Just quit this bullshit of calling at the last minute, and giving excuses."

"If I could make it, I would but, truthfully, I think I have a big story on the hook, and I don't want someone else to get it. This is front page, above the fold."

"Fuck your fold, and the newspaper that goes with it," and she hangs up.

Bob puts the phone down, looks across the room, and spots the new girl who has recently joined the paper from some Richmond, VA-area throw-away. He walks over and asks, "Sue, is it?"

She stares at him, and answers, "Yes. Call me Sue, please."

"Look, if you're not real busy, could you give me a hand researching some information that Ralph needs yesterday?"

"What information?"

"I need to get a list of all the names of the victims of drive-by shootings that took place over the last five years. That was an extraordinary time, because of all the gang wars going on, but I need any names that you can come up with. As soon as you have any, get them over to me, and I'll do some follow-up on them. Are you okay with that?"

"Sure, we can look all of that up on the new computer program. It shouldn't take me very long. I'll get right back to you."

"Thanks, I appreciate it."

Forty minutes later, Sue walks over to Bob's desk as he's finishing his evening story of the double murder he's been covering for the evening news.

"Thirty-six."

"Thirty-six?"

"Thirty-six drive-by killings over the last five years. None solved, no arrests, all in the dead file."

"Christ, this will take weeks to figure out."

"Maybe not," says Sue. "The new program broke them down by gang members or civilians. Most were gang members. Most likely we're talking about some civilian who lost his kid."

Bob says, "So, for the sake of time, let's eliminate the gang members that were shot, and concentrate on the civilians. Make a list with their names and addresses and let's take a ride out to speak to them. One of them just might be our kidnapper. I'll be right back. I'll tell Ralph what we're doing."

WBAL has a computer system that quickly picked up the same information that *The Sun* had. The problem was that the intern who was trying to assimilate the information for the station was not as computer literate as Sue at *The Sun*. Consequently, while he was scrambling to discover how many drive-by murders took place over the last few years, Sue was preparing the list of people to see with Bob Turner. When Turner returns to Sue's desk, the list is complete, she's made two copies, and hands one to him.

"So, who's first?" she asks, as she grabs her purse.

Turner, looking over the list of seventeen names, says, "Let's start with the closest, and work our way out to the suburbs. Do you have a tape recorder with you, just in case?"

Sue looks in her large purse, and pulls out a small recorder. She opens her desk drawer, takes out a couple fresh batteries, and slides them into her purse. "I don't want to run out of power."

By the time they had seen just three of the families listed, it was lunchtime, and the two of them were emotionally drained from hearing their stories. There was no doubt, in either of their minds, that any one of these three families had every reason to seek revenge. However, both of them agreed that they didn't seem like the kind of people who would go around kidnapping children to prove their point.

Bob stopped near the Inner Harbor Place, where he knew they could grab a quick bite. The area was packed, but he knew exactly where to park so that he didn't get a ticket. They ended up getting hot dogs from a street vendor, and sitting outside on one of the benches, looking out over the Bay.

"Nice view," says Sue.

"You'll get used to it. Baltimore can grow on you. I've been here all my life and watched it change. Most of the change came about with the Harbor Place, and the Orioles Baseball stadium development. Have you had an opportunity to see the city?"

"Only a small part, as I do my job covering weddings, funerals, and some local council meetings. What surprised me most, was how spread out the city is. If it weren't for the freeway system, it would take forever to get from one place to the other. Luckily, I found an apartment just on the other side of Druid Park. It can be a little hairy at night, but I haven't run into any problems so far."

"What makes it so hairy?"

"There are a couple bars, on either end of the block, that draw some weird customers late at night. The building I'm in has a garage that I rent, so I don't have to park on the street but, many early mornings, the police sirens wake me. Other than that, it's a pretty decent neighborhood. I know several of my neighbors have complained to the police to close the bars, or make them close earlier, but to no avail. I guess it's part of living in the big city."

"I thought you lived down in Richmond. That's a pretty fair-sized town."

"Actually, I lived just outside downtown, near the University of Virginia, with my parents, who were born and raised in that area. My dad is a teacher; my mom is a lawyer. I have two brothers who are also lawyers, and work in D.C."

"Don't all the lawyers around the Capital work in D.C.?"

She smiled. "Pretty much, I guess. They have been successful with their little firm, and both live in Alexandria with their families. I'm the baby of my family."

"You don't look like a baby," he quickly says, looking at her from top to bottom.

She laughs, and says, "Are you hitting on me?"

"I wasn't, but that doesn't mean I won't."

Again, she laughs and asks, "You sure that's just a Pepsi you're drinking?"

CHAPTER 47

As they drive to the next name on the list, Bob has his mind on Sue, and how she has handled herself today. He recognizes her quick mind, easy interview style, and how the three previous visits were made easier by having her with him. She seems to put the families at ease, even when they are so distraught that tears came pouring down their faces. He wonders just how old she is, thinking she must be in her late twenties, having interned in Richmond for five years before coming into Baltimore, plus finishing college. Hell, I'm not that much older then she is. Well, maybe a little. But, I haven't reached the big 4-0 yet.

Because of traffic, they only manage to see two more families during the afternoon, with similar results. Bob would love a drink, and says to Sue, "I could sure use a drink, care to join me?"

"I thought you'd never ask," she responds. "I never imagined just how painful it is to lose someone in a drive-by, and know that you'll probably never get closure. However, I can understand the problem the police have in trying to run down the shooters. No one is going to put their ass on the line to finger gang members. It's just too risky."

"It is," says Bob, "But if someone, sometime, doesn't do it, then these type of ridiculous killings will continue. What I've always thought was a good idea is what the British do in London. They have cameras on all the streets and can go back to them immediately, find the car, and follow it wherever it goes. That's probably why they don't have the same problem we do."

"You ought to run for Mayor, maybe we can get that done," she says.

"I'll pass, thanks."

They arrive in front of a cute restaurant called "Blown Away," and Bob parks his car. They go inside and Sue sees that the place is divided into two rooms, one a bar and the other a restaurant. It's still early, so they are the only ones at the bar. Turning to Sue, Bob asks, "You are 21, aren't you?"

"A hell of a way to get me to tell you how old I am. I passed that goal 10 years ago, but thanks for the compliment."

The bartender comes over and takes their orders. Both ask for beer, and Bob asks for a bowl of peanuts and a bowl of pretzels.

"You've obviously been here before," says Sue.

"Just a few hundred times. My house is just up the block."

"Nice neighborhood, but expensive isn't it?"

"I made some money in the stock market, and decided to

buy the house rather than wait until I was too old to enjoy it. It was a great investment, since I took my money out of the market just before the crash in ' 08. The prices now are probably double what I paid, and the neighborhood keeps improving. When I moved here this restaurant was a dingy place, but was bought out by a couple of nerds who made their money in the dot-com industry. They've done a wonderful job, as you can see and, believe me, in an hour or so, this place will be packed."

"How's the food?"

"Really good. Would you like to have dinner?"

"After that hot dog this afternoon, I could use some decent food."

"Wait here, I'll be right back."

Bob reserves a quiet booth, in the back of the restaurant, and comes back to the bar. "The restaurant won't be open to the public for an hour or so. Why don't you finish your drink and we can wait over at my place?"

"Sounds like a plan," she responds.

The house is a three-story brownstone, with marble steps leading to the front door. As they enter, she notices that she can see straight through the house, to what looks like the kitchen. On her right is the living room, furnished with very contemporary pieces, and large framed posters of Broadway plays along one wall. He walks her towards the back of the house, through a very nice dining room, and then as she had surmised, into the kitchen. It was very modern and clean, which surprised her.

"Who's your housekeeper? The place is immaculate."

"Thanks! That's me. I've been told I'm very anal about the place, but to tell you the truth, I love being here, so I keep the place the way I want it. Come on, I'll show you the best part of the house."

He opens a door next to the kitchen and they walk down to the basement, or what she would have assumed was the basement. However, at the bottom of the stairs is a large carpeted room, with knotty pine walls and recessed lighting. Towards the back of the room is a large pool table and, against the back wall, is a bar with a large mirror behind it. The front of the room has three leather chairs facing a sofa, and what looks like a 60" or 70" TV mounted on the wall.

"Jesus, a man cave."

"Every Sunday, when the Ravens play, this place is packed with friends. It is my pride and joy. You like it?"

"I love it! Hell, I have to watch the games on a small TV in my apartment."

"Well, officially, I am inviting you to become one of the gang. So whenever you want to watch the Ravens, just come on over."

"Thanks, I just might take you up on that."

"So, let's climb the mountain and see the rest of the place."

They get up to the second floor, which has two large bedrooms and two large bathrooms . The master bedroom is in the back of the house because, as Bob explains, there's no traffic noise back here.

Sue asks, "Would you mind if I used the bathroom down the hall? I'd like to wash up before dinner."

"You can shower in there if you want. There are robes hanging there, for company, and I unfortunately don't have much company. I'm going to go down to my cave and get a glass of wine. You want one?"

"Sure, that would be great." Looking at the enormous bathroom and tiled shower, she asks, "You sure you wouldn't mind my taking a shower?"

"Be my guest, really."

Bob heads downstairs and Sue undresses. She loves the place and would never have imagined Bob living in a home like this. She has had her eye on him, since she arrived at *The Sun*, but was told he was seeing someone, so she backed off.

She hasn't had a good shower since her last trip home. Her apartment's shower is so cruddy that even the best cleanser only gets the surface dirt off. Seeing all the goodies along the wall of the shower, including some very expensive-looking shampoo, she decides to go for the full treatment and washes her hair first, then showers. As she dries off, there is a knock at the door.

"You okay in there, or do I need to call the police?"

She laughs and says, "I'm fine. I'm better than fine. I'll be right out."

She puts on one of the thick bathrobes hanging on the back of the door, puts some make up on, brushes her hair, and opens the door.

Bob isn't there so she walks downstairs to the first floor, and then down to the man cave. Luckily the cave is carpeted, since she didn't have slippers to wear, and couldn't find any in the bathroom.

Bob is sitting in one of the leather chairs watching the news, and drinking a glass of wine, when she arrives. He gets up and hands her the glass of red he had poured for her. Then he turns off the TV, and turns on a stereo system that fills the room with soft jazz.

"I can't believe this place."

"Thanks. By the way, if you want, I can turn the heat on down here to warm the place up."

She takes a sip of the wine and says, "I'm O.K."

Bob, who has been thinking about her in his shower, and now staring at her in the robe that she's almost wearing, says, "This is undoubtedly the wrong thing to say, and probably will get me fired but, I'd like to make love to you."

She stops drinking, thinks about what he just said for a second, then stands up, drops her robe, and asks, "Here or upstairs?"

An hour later, as she straddles him on his bed, she looks into his eyes and says, "Is this what they mean by 'fucking your way to the top'?"

Bob cracks up, and she joins in, and they both laugh until they cry.

Finally, Bob says, "You're fantastic, you know that? In a million years I could never imagine you here with me in this bed. Your body is exquisite and, candidly, I'm exhausted."

Leaning over, she kisses him and says, "Enough with the sweet talk. Take me out to dinner, I'm starving."

CHAPTER 48

———— ⌇⌇ ————

At 2:45 p.m., Jeff's car turns into the driveway. He waits for the garage door to open, and pulls in. He eases out of the car, which is difficult because of his height. When he enters the kitchen he heads for the refrigerator, to get a beer, and is confronted by Pat, holding a gun in his face. He's about to say something, when he notices the others all in the room, all with guns pointed at him. He relaxes, and asks, "OK, what's going on?"

Manuel says, "Nothing much, Jeff. We were told today that you were cutting us off and, now, we decided to cut you out. We want your list of contacts. You get the picture, you asshole?"

Jeff, sensing the anger, decides to see if he can talk to them. "Look, this is wrong. Each of you became successful because of me, and my contacts. You've all had a good life, and expanded all over Baltimore. I never questioned how you did your business, even when you were all killing each other a few years ago. I've kept it strictly business. There's never been a complaint, all these years, and all of you," looking around the room at the young men, "know that I've never cheated on an ounce, and you all know that. So now, your business is slow, you want to cut me out of the picture. Look, I need to move the merchandise that's in my warehouse. All of you understand that. I can't get more unless I pay for what I received. This is not a credit business, and the people I buy from do not care if your business is slow or not. They want the money from the products you sell."

"What you're doing is irresponsible. Plus, the Mexican cartel won't work with you, they don't even know you exist, other than through me. They don't even know who you are, for Christ's sake, nor do they care. If I disappear, they'd likely send a cadre of their killers up here and clean you all out. Believe me, you don't want to piss them off."

Finally, Rick, who is standing in front of Jeff and still pointing his gun at him says, "Jeff, between our families, we control most of fucking Baltimore and the surrounding towns. We have over 250 men working for us, and that's not counting the kids that sell the merchandise on the streets. We have enough fucking weapons to start the Third World War. You think the cartel will want to do that? You think they won't want to come up here and negotiate a new and better deal with us? Come on Jeff, you're a big boy. Give us the fucking information and you live. Don't, and you will take a very long time to fucking die. One way or the other, the cartel will end up dealing with us, you understand?"

Jeff takes a pack of cigarettes out of his shirt pocket,

giving him a moment to think. He owes the cartel around $20 million, for the merchandise sitting in the warehouse, which is due to be paid this week. They expect to be paid on time. He has never missed a payment, and he doesn't want to start now. He has over $35 million dollars in various banks, most offshore, that he could use if he had to. He wished he could get to his warehouse, but the likelihood of that happening is remote.

He says, "Let's all take a second to go into the living room, sit down, and discuss this." He walks past Ricky, and they all follow him. His home is on the Chesapeake, and the view from the living room is spectacular.

Once they are all seated, Jeff says, "Between you, and the other families, I need to get the $20 million owed to me. That's as a starter. If you want to control the drug import from Mexico, fine. They won't even discuss it until they are paid. They get very unhappy with excuses. So first, get together the money to pay for the merchandise in my warehouse. Otherwise, you can kill me and you'll still have just enough merchandise to cover you for the short term, and nowhere to get more."

"Now," Jeff said while looking around the room, "if you still want to take over my distribution once you pay the bill, and get the merchandise out of the warehouse, then I'll contact the cartel, and switch the business over to you."

They look at each other and Ricky says, "Tie the motherfucker up and let's talk."

After they tie him up, and drop him next to his housekeeper, they meet in what seems to be his den. They go over to his desk, and open the box sitting on it. Inside are fresh Cuban cigars. They each take one, and light them up.

Manuel says, "Now this is more like it. Let's figure this out."

"Too many loose ends," says Ricky. "He gets our money, pays off the cartel, and then forgets about the whole deal."

Manuel says, "I've been thinking the same thing, so how about we have him call the cartel from here, and tell them what's going down the way he told us? Then we agree to pay, as long as he takes off. Once he tells the cartel who we are, and we talk to them and tell them what we can do for them, they won't need him. They must speak English, because I don't think Jeff speaks Spanish, so we all will understand what's happening."

They all agree. They march back into the kitchen and tell Jeff what's going to happen. He agrees to make the call, and does. It doesn't take long for the people on the other end of the phone, and there are a number listening and talking, sometimes all at once, to understand just what's going down.

Once Manuel begins to talk to them in Spanish, they agree that the transfer of leadership is a good idea, as long as their $20 million is sent to them this week, as usual. They tell Jeff to give the five of them the information right away. Once everyone agrees, the cartel spokesperson says, "We'll see how well you do with this new shipment, and then we'll talk again next month."

After they get off the phone Pat looks at Jeff and says, "$20 million, isn't that what you said? So, sit down and start writing out the list of contacts and sources, and especially the people who you pay off for protection. Then, after you contact each one of them, tell them you're retiring and give them our names to contact, we're going down to my bank and have you quitclaim this home over to us. I like the place, and the neighborhood."

Manuel gives Pat a small punch in the shoulder, and they all laugh. As he finishes, he notices that Ricky takes his cell out to answer a call.

"No kidding? Okay, I'll tell them." The TV reported a story that the person taking our kids is someone who's looking for revenge, because his kid was killed in a drive-by. He called the TV station, and gave them the information without leaving his name."

Pat asks, "What we going to do about it? You know he wouldn't leave his name. However, the station might have caught his telephone number in their system, and back-checked it for his name. I think someone has to go down to the station and have a heart to heart with them."

Manuel says, "There's probably an army of cops down there already. How about calling Murphy, and see if he has any information he can give us? He's been pretty straight with us so far."

"Do it," says Pat.

"Murphy," answers Brian, from his cell phone.

"Lieutenant, Manuel Diaz. I just heard that some creep called the TV station and said that the kids were taken because of some revenge he wanted."

"That's true, Manuel. We are following up on that lead, and hope to have his name soon."

"How soon?"

"Manuel, I won't lie to you. It's going to take manpower to go through the archives of dead cases to find this guy, but we will. I have a number of additional officers called in to help."

"What about the TV station? They got the call. Their switchboard should have the number and, if they do, you can call the telephone company and get his address."

"We've already been through that. The guy not only called the TV station, he also called *The Sun*, and gave them the same story. The problem is, he used a burner phone, just like you fellas do. It's impossible to track it down. No, this one's going to take legwork on our part, and we've already begun. Believe me Manuel, we want him as much as you do."

"Difference is, Lieutenant, we want him dead."

"I understand, but let us try it our way. You getting involved will only mess up the arrest. Please tell everyone to keep out of it, for the time being. We think this is coming to an end."

"Okay for now but, don't take too long. You know what I mean?"

"I get you. Thanks, Manuel."

The gang leaders are furious. They hate the man who took their kids, they hate the cops and, right now, they hate Jeff. They are being pounded, by their respective families, to get the kidnapper and do to him what he might have done to their children. They all need to get back to their families; however, first they need to untie the old lady, who has been there all afternoon. Once they had sent her on her way, with a warning to keep her mouth shut, they sit down, with the now exhausted Jeff, and have him make the calls.

When they finish, Pat takes one last draw on the cigar he's smoking, and says to Jeff, "It's been a pleasure working with you. By the way, I really don't want this place. Too many rich people around."

They all laugh, except Jeff.

One by one the gang leaders head out the door to their respective cars. Jeff gets himself a drink, from the bar in his den, and sits down. Looking out at the Bay, he realizes that he's shaking from the experience. Fuck them, he thinks. They'll probably end up killing each other over the territories within a year. He swallows a mouthful of scotch, and begins to settle down. I'll miss this place, he thinks, but there are plenty of other homes around the world I can enjoy. Who would have thought those fuckers would pull something like this on me?

Finally, after having a second drink, Jeff decides to shower. During the entire time he was tied up, he'd been thinking about the next moves he has to make to transition into his retirement mode. It will take him a day or two, to get his business affairs in order, but he could do that from his place outside of Paris.

As Jeff walks out of the shower, he sees a gun pointed at his head. Before he can scream, his head explodes, and he drops down onto the tile floor. The shooter bends down, to make sure he's dead, and says, "Nobody retires."

As the shooter leaves the room, two men walk in, wrap the body in a large plastic sheet, and carry him out to his garage. They open the garage door, back their old Buick sedan into the garage, and drop his body into the trunk. They then drive to a junk yard, just inside the Virginia State line, and pull right up to the compactor. Within minutes the large car is lifted onto the platform, and the crushing begins.

Once completed, the smashed piece of steel, with Jeff's remains inside, is tossed onto a large pile of junk, and ready to be exported to China.

CHAPTER 49

After dinner they finished off a bottle of Pinot Noir, and then Bob and Sue headed back to Bob's place where they tore at each other's clothes, going up the stairs, and were naked by the time they made it to the bed. For the next half hour, they went at each other like two cats in heat. They only stopped because Bob got a cramp in his leg.

"Jesus, you're killing me," he says, rubbing the back of his leg.

Sue, naked, is sitting up against the headboard smoking a cigarette. Watching him squeeze the tightness out of the back of his leg, she says, "I've been thinking about these kidnappings."

"When?" he asks, looking over at her.

She laughs and says, "Not when we were having sex. Believe me, it took all my concentration for that dance. No, just now."

"Alright, so what have you got for me?"

"I think you mean, 'What have I got for us?.' I expect a full byline for this action."

He laughs in pain, "Lady, you sure know how to grab a guy by the balls. So tell me, what do you have to share?"

"Revenge is really personal, and kidnapping small kids would suggest that the revenge he or she is seeking has to do with the loss of a child. If that's true, we can eliminate all but three of the rest of these names."

"You know what? You deserve a byline if this proves out. That's brilliant."

"I agree," she responds. "Now, if you have some lotion in the house, tell me where, and I'll give your leg a good rub-down to get rid of the cramp. Plus, if you're lucky, I might rub other parts of your body...but I'm afraid it probably won't relax you."

Early the next morning, after they made love again and showered, they drove over to Sue's so she could change her clothes. Then, they decided to visit the three remaining people on their list who would qualify under Sue's criteria as person or persons who might have an axe to grind. The closest one was in Pikesville, the next in Stevenson. They chose to go to Pikesville first, where they stopped and had a wonderful breakfast of lox, bagels, and eggs. They finished their coffee, and headed out to see the first family.

They did not call first, hoping to catch them unaware, as they did with the others they had visited. The first stop proved a bad call. The father of the child who had been killed was blind, his wife was an invalid, and they lived quietly on a side street with a caretaker.

The drive out to Stevenson was a lovely ride. The streets were lined with trees, and the homes were beautiful. The grounds on some of the properties looked like they belonged in *Better Homes and Gardens*. There were a few gardeners working on properties. Sue couldn't imagine how there could be so many wealthy people in this one area.

When they arrived at the Teller home, it was 11:00 a.m. The home seemed quiet, and no lights were showing either downstairs or up. They approached the home and rang the bell. They waited for a minute, and rang the bell again. Finally, they heard some movement behind the door. When the door swung open, they were facing an old man, wearing a shirt and slacks too big for him.

"Yes?" he said.

Sue, looking down at her notebook, asked, "Mr. Teller?"

"Yes, how can I help you?"

Bob says, "We're from *The Baltimore Sun* and would like to ask you a few questions, if you have the time."

Ed stepped aside and said, "Come in, please."

They follow him into a very large living room with two sofas facing each other, and easy chairs all around the room. The colors are tasteful and subdued.

"Can I get you something to drink?" Ed asks.

"No thanks," Bob responds.

"We just have a couple questions that need to be cleared up."

"Please, go ahead," says Teller.

Bob begins, "Have you been following the kidnappings in the city, sir?"

"Oh, yes. Indeed I have."

"Is it true your son was shot to death in downtown, about three years ago, in a drive-by shooting?"

Ed's face quickly expresses his pain, which both Sue and Bob pick up on.

"Yes," he says.

Sue says, "If this is too painful for you to discuss, we can come back some other time."

"No, no," Ed quickly says. "Some pain never goes away, and coming back would just prolong it."

"Prolong what, Mr. Teller?"

"Prolong the inevitable, young man. Prolong the inevitable."

Sue asks, "Could you explain what you mean, sir?"

"I can, but first I need a glass of water. Would either of you like some water?"

Both say yes, and follow him into the kitchen.

Ed pulls down three glasses, then goes to the refrigerator, and brings out a container of cold water. He fills the glasses, takes a drink from one, and hands the others to Bob and Sue. He walks back into the living room carrying his glass, as well as the container of water, and sits down.

Ed says, "I'm very impressed with the two of you. I wish our police force was as competent, and followed up as well. I called your paper yesterday, expecting very little would be done to find the caller, since that's the experience I have had in the past." He takes a sip of the water, and continues.

"Have either of you had a member of your family murdered?"

They look at each other and Sue says, "Not me." Bob repeats her words.

"Then this whole situation will seem rather foreign to the two of you. You see, my son was murdered in front of my wife almost three years ago. He was 10 years old, and our only child. She had to be institutionalized.One second, please."

He gets up, goes over to the piano, picks up a photo, and brings it over to them. "That was my son. A truly beautiful child, who could not have been more of a blessing to his parents if he tried."

Ed, who is trying to hold it together, breaks down and begins to cry. Sue immediately gets up, sits next to him, and puts her arm around him while saying, "Please take your time, Mr. Teller. This must be excruciating. We have all the time in the world. Can I get you anything other than the water?"

Ed wipes his tears on his handkerchief and says, "Thank you, young lady. You are very kind, but I need to finish my story," and he does.

It is almost two o'clock when he finishes. Sue's eyes are red from crying, and Bob finally turns off the tape machine and says, "Ed, what do you want to do? You understand that the police will find you, and God only knows what will happen. However, even worse, the gangs might find you and you really don't want that to happen, believe me. I have witnessed what they do to people they are angry with."

"I am guilty of some very awful things. I understand that I have to face the public, and explain what I have done. I have already hired an outstanding lawyer, who will help me through the process. I thought I'd throw the media a bone, in hopes that I could get the public involved in this case before they see and hear all the horrific things that I have done. In a way, that has happened through the TV broadcast. I was hoping that it would last a few more days. However, smiling at the two of them, "I didn't expect the two of you to show up so quickly. I'm open to suggestions."

"Being selfish, I'd like to hide you somewhere for the next few days, so I can get the story out and sell some papers. However, I've been around long enough to know that WBAL may be as close to discovering you as we were. If they are, so are the police and the gangs. My recommendation would be that you call the police, and confess. We can stay here with you, to help ensure your safety, or you can call your lawyer to join you. I just believe the sooner you move on this, the better. It probably won't change the results, but at least you'll be safe."

Sue and Bob wait while Ed makes his decision. They are both hyped over the entire interview, and pained by what Ed has been going through. But, murder is murder, and they both know he has no chance of beating the charge.

Finally, Ed looks up and says, "You're right Bob. I'm going to call the police., I might as well close this out now."

"I have the phone number for the local police station. It's better that you call them, than 911, where the Maryland State Police will respond."

Bob gives Ed the number, and he makes the call. Bob and Sue wonder what will happen when the police come and find them. Sue waits until Ed has finished his call and says, "Ed, would you mind if we call this story in, before the police come and throw us out?"

Ed says, "Of course not. Please go ahead. You can use my office, just on the other side of the kitchen."

They hear the first police cars arrive, just as they had finished giving their story to *The Sun*. Ed, seeing the cars begin to surround his home, says to the two of them, "Thank you for what you've done. I guess I clearly didn't think about how this would end, as thoroughly as I thought I had."

Bob says, "Ed, we'll be there for you throughout the trial. Please call us if we might be able to help with anything."

As Ed says thanks, a knock comes on the front door.

CHAPTER 50

———⁓⁓⁓———

Brian had been driving back to his office when his cell phone rang. He pulled over, and answered.

"Lt. Murphy."

"Lieutenant, the duty officer just had a call from some guy claiming he's the one who took the kids. We thought he was just another nut, but he began to tell some details that made him take the information and call me."

"What's the man's name and address?'

He gave them to Brian, who recognized the Stevenson area, and told the sergeant to call an all-points, and surround that home until he arrived. "No one, and I mean no one, is to approach him until I arrive. Is that clear?"

"Absolutely. I'm on it."

Brian put his flasher on, and raced out to Stevenson. He arrived there 13 minutes later and saw police cars all around the neighborhood. He pulled up to the closest car and noticed Sam Delgado, a sergeant he knew.

"Care to take a walk with me, Sam?"

The sergeant smiled at Brian and climbed out of the car, checking his revolver. He went to the trunk of his car and took out two bulletproof vests. He tossed one to Brian, who put it on under his jacket. The two of them approach the front door and knock, moving to the sides of the door. The door opens, and a man around 70 answers, and asks them in. They wait for him to go first, and follow.

He walks into his beautifully appointed living room and asks, "Can I get either of you a drink? Coffee, tea?"

Brian, staring directly at him, says, "I don't think so."

Just then, Brian sees Bob and Sue. He recognizes Bob Turner and says loudly, "What are you doing here?!" Brian turns to Teller and says, "Mr. Teller, can you explain why they are here?"

"Yes, I can but, first let me say, I'm the one who called. I took those children. It was me. No one else. And I take full responsibility for it."

Brian looks back at the two reporters and again asks, "What the hell are you doing here?!"

He turns back to Teller and asks, "Where are the children?"

"Oh, they are all resting in peace," answers Ed.

Brian, still looking directly at Ed, asks, "What do mean 'resting in peace,' Mr. Teller?"

"Before I answer you, I want to tell you why I took the children. So, why don't you two sit down? This will take a while."

"Mr. Teller," says Brian, "I need to know where those

children are, and whether or not you hurt them. I need to know now."

"Lieutenant, if you want to find those children, you'll sit down and listen. Otherwise, you can leave now and never find them. So, what's it going to be?"

Brian looks over to Sam, who shrugs. Before he sits down, he looks at the two reporters and says, "Unless you two had something to do with this crime, you better get your butts out of here." He walks them out to the front, calls over an officer, and says, "lock them in the back of your car, and make sure they don't leave."

He goes back into the living room and sits down. Brian keeps his eyes directed at Teller. "I'm going to turn on this recorder," the sergeant says, pulling out a compact recorder from his pocket. Sam states clearly into the recorder, "This is Sergeant Sam Delgado, with Lt. Brian Murphy, interviewing Mr. Ed Teller. Mr. Teller has volunteered to speak to us about the disappearance of the children in downtown Baltimore. Have I stated the reason we are here correctly, Mr. Teller?" He pushes the recorder a little closer to Teller.

Teller waits until the recorder is set up on the table before him and says, "Yes, this is my statement and it is voluntary."

"This began a couple years ago."

An hour later, when Teller finishes his story, Sam puts the tape recorder back in his pocket. Brian asks the sergeant to cuff Teller.

Sam pulls Teller's arms behind his back, cuffs him, and leads him out to the police car.

Brian gets on the phone and tells his station sergeant to get several cars and ambulances down to Lake Drive. He gives them the details and says "Try to keep this just within our station, so none of the families hear about it until we personally tell them what happened. I don't want them around that house right now. It's going to become a zoo as it is."

Brian walks over to Sam's police car and tells him to take Teller downtown, to the station. He also asks him to drop the tape recorder off as evidence, and to make a copy of the confession for him.

"By the way, I appreciate your help, sergeant." The sergeant looks in the back seat, at Teller, and says, "Lieutenant, I thought I'd seen it all, after 20 years on the force, but this one takes the cake."

Thinking about solving the disappearances of the six children, in the home on Lake Drive, Brian at once feels elated, and incredibly depressed at the same time. My God, what is this world coming to? This is not some monster who enjoys the sight of dead kids. This is an educated, wealthy man, who is hurt beyond belief. He wanted revenge. Revenge because we, the police department, fucked up and never found the person who killed his kid. I can just hear the defense attorney pleading for mercy. I think I'll call Terry, and ask him to come with me on these calls. There are going to be a lot of angry people in the city tonight. Once Teller tells his tale to the press, the whole town's going to take sides. What does Sally always say? "And this too, shall pass."

CHAPTER 51

Bob and Sue are sitting in the back of the police car. Both are quiet.

Finally, Sue asks, "When do you get used to it?"

Bob, who is still caught up with Ed Teller's confession, is startled by her voice, and responds, "Used to what?"

"The stories, the killings, the heartache, the futility. He broke my heart listening to how much he loved that child of his, and his wife. It happened so quickly. One minute you're in paradise, the next in hell. How does one cope with that kind of trauma?"

"I don't have any answers. I've seen some ugly murders over the years, right here in Baltimore, including kids shooting kids, and husbands killing wives. I write the stories; I don't create them. They create themselves. Just like Teller. He had many roads he could have taken. He chose the wrong one. You're going to find yourself caught up in this situation over and over, if you want to remain a reporter. But by definition, you are a reporter, you're the messenger, nothing more. You tell the public the facts, and let them find meaning in the words you write. You don't tell them how to feel or react. That's on them. Does it mean you can't be sympathetic? Of course not. However, you need to always be objective when you put the words to paper. That's your job. That's my job. Will you stop crying when you hear stories like Teller's? I doubt it. Believe me, it pays to count to ten, get away from the incident, and then think about what happened, how it happened, why it happened, and to whom it happened. Then, write the damned story from only the facts. Leave the tears in your handkerchief."

"I'm not sure I'll ever be that objective," she says.

"It takes time and experience. It takes looking at dead bodies lying on the street with bullet holes in them, and noticing the person isn't wearing a ring, or has only one sock on. Those are the weird things I look for, because the body needs to speak to someone, and it's either going to be me, or the cops, or the mortician. But only I can convey the effect of that body to the public, in a way they understand and feel something...anything. That's the job I love because, when the story is right and the public calls in and expresses its gratitude for the article, you know you are a reporter. We can't do a damned thing for Teller except tell his story, as he told it to us, and hope the public begins to understand what was in his twisted mind as he killed those kids. That's our job."

Looking over at her, he continues, "And, it's under our byline that the article will be published, so get used to being famous, because you're about to experience fame like you never thought possible."

Brian then opens the back door of the police car, with Bob and Sue in it, and demands, "I'll ask you one more time. What were you two doing in Teller's home?"

"We had followed up on a call to the paper yesterday, which we discovered came from Teller. We had already gone to, and eliminated, other people whose relatives were killed in drive-by shootings. When we arrived here, Teller invited us in, and spilled the beans. He was just waiting for someone to confess to, and we got here first."

"I shouldn't ask, but did either one of you record his confession?"

Sue takes out her small recorder, and hands it over to Brian.

"I'll get this back to you after the trial," Brian says.

"That's okay, Lieutenant, I have others. Plus, I downloaded the entire transcript before you arrived. So, you can keep it."

Brian looks at her, shakes his head, and says, "Try not to make this guy sound too nice. He murdered six kids by pulling plastic bags over their heads. He's not a hero. Now get the hell out of here."

CHAPTER 52

Terry is going through folders Sol had given him, describing in detail the various enterprises Sol is associated with, as well as all the important people that are connected to those enterprises. Sol wasn't kidding when he said it would take years to absorb all this information.

His cellphone rings, and Terry picks up. "Terry Stein."

"Terry, Brian. You busy?"

"Not if you need to talk."

"We have the man responsible for the missing downtown kids."

"Really? Congratulations. Boy, that was quick."

"Terry, he killed them all. Six in total."

"Oh, damned! I'm sorry, Brian. What can I do?"

"I'm heading downtown to talk to the families in person, before they hear it from the press. If you aren't too busy, I'd love to have you with me. It's going to be rough."

"Pick me up. I'll wait for your call, and meet you downstairs. I'll tell Monica where I'll be, and that it will probably take some time."

Terry hangs up and calls Monica. She answers, "Terry, how sweet."

"It's not a social call, I'm afraid."

"What's the matter, sweetheart?"

"I just heard from Brian. They've caught the man who took the children."

"Well, that's wonderful. Please give Brian my best for getting this done so quickly. I'm sure the city will be pleased."

"They're all dead, Monica. He killed six kids."

Her cry was audible. "I'm sorry to tell you like this," said Terry, "but Brian has asked me to help him break the news to the families. You going to be okay?"

Crying, and wiping the tears from her face, she answers, "Go. I'll be okay, but come home as soon as you can."

"I promise. I love you, you know."

"I know. Just be careful."

On the way downtown, Brian tells Terry the whole story. Like Brian, Terry feels as if the system has let Ed Teller down. However, he says, "That's no excuse for causing other families to go through the same thing he experienced. It should have given him more compassion for those who lose their children. My God! Six small defenseless children, gone. I think, when we present the news to the families, we should begin with the story of his losing his son in a gang-related gun fight, just downstairs from his office. I'm not sure that will make them feel better, but they need to understand that what they do has consequences. We don't need to rub their noses in it. However, telling them the truth now is better than them reading about it in the newspapers, or seeing it on TV. This was a case of revenge, pure and simple. I'm sure that's the way the news media will play it. By the way, maybe you should call ahead, and tell the families to meet at one location. They can all hear the bad news at the same time, and be there to support each other, rather than blame each other."

Brian picks up his phone and, handing it to Terry, says, "All the numbers are listed, call while I'm driving. It's a good idea and, hearing it from you might get them motivated to stop shooting each other. Although, I doubt it."

CHAPTER 53

Brian and Terry stop for coffee before going to Ricky's sister's place, which was determined after a number of Terry's calls to get everyone to agree to meet. He had not been able to contact the leaders of the families but, was assured they would be at the meeting that afternoon. While they ate, Brian gets a phone call from the coroner.

"We found them just as he said we would. They were all lying in the basement of one of the houses on Lake Drive. They all had plastic bags tied over their heads, as you said, and were wrapped in sheets of plastic. The place smelled awful. I doubt any of the kids suffered for very long. We took lots of pictures, especially the sign on the wall behind them, saying in foot high letters, 'Revenge.' Each of the bodies also had a picture of Teller's wife and kid attached to their clothes. It breaks your heart, the whole damned thing."

"I agree. Clean the place out after you get the evidence

wrapped up, and take pictures of everything. The press show yet?"

"Amazingly, no. I can't believe we've been able to keep a lid on this for two hours. But, who's complaining?"

"Thanks Doc. I'll see you later." Brian turns to Terry and says, "Looks like he was telling the truth."

"Sometimes, I wonder what the hell is the truth?" says Terry.

The meeting is as predictable as they expected. The parents were inconsolable. The gang leaders asked if they could get ahold of Teller for five minutes, in a room. Brian was happy to have Terry there to defuse some of the anger but, he knew that once the papers began to describe the cellar, and the way Teller killed their children, all hell would break loose at City Hall. The two of them left three hours later. Terry asked Brian to drop him off at Monica's. He asked Brian if he wanted to have dinner with them. Brian declined, and said he had to finish this up. He had to go to the morgue, and then write the whole case up for the DA. He knew how important the paperwork would be for the trial.

Brian dropped Terry off at his apartment building, and headed to the office. Terry opened the door of their apartment and called out to Monica. There was no response. He went into the kitchen and saw a large note on the counter, where they have left each other messages in the past. It said, "Heading over to the conference room, for meeting with partners and pizza dinner at 7:00. Try and make it." He looked at his watch. 6:35. He had enough time to shower, change, and get over there by 7:30. He called Monica, told her he had just gotten home, and that he would be there by 7:30. She was delighted, and told him to hurry.

When he arrives, the six of them, including Michael Tourney, the accountant, are sitting around the conference table looking at a large map of the proposed development. It seems larger than when Terry had seen it before. It is covered with marks where everyone had been scribbling. There are three large pizzas at the end of the table, and beer and water bottles as well. Monica comes over and gives Terry a kiss and tells him she is happy he is back. She whispers, "Everything go okay?"

He whispers back "As well as could be expected. I'll tell you more when we get home."

She says, "We now have a new partnership. Ralph's firm will do the paperwork. And, we agreed to keep the equity of the original name, and call it 4 Baltimore, Inc."

She tells him what Ralph's father has suggested, and Terry is delighted. He joins them around the map, and tries to learn what it's going to be like to be a real estate developer. While they put their creativity together for the development, Brian works on the detailed paperwork, which he knows will be the basis for the Teller trial. He works until midnight, when his body screams out to leave so, he closes his computer, and heads home. He arrives expecting Sally to still be with their daughter but, instead, finds her in bed reading.

Sally says, "Do I know you?"

He laughs with her, and goes over to give her a kiss. He

loves the taste of her lips, and the fresh smell she seems to always have. He sits on the edge of the bed and asks, "So how are the two beauties?"

"Bridget is fine. Sore, but fine. It was rather an easy birth. And the baby, what can I say? She's a doll. I've already signed her up for the Miss America Pageant."

"Is Scott home with her?"

"Actually, a nurse was there. Scott hired her for tonight. It seems he and Andrew had an important meeting with Terry and Monica tonight."

"That's funny. I spent the entire afternoon with Terry. I wish he had told me he had the meeting, we could have returned earlier."

"He's a big boy, Brian. If he felt he needed to be some-where else, he would have told you. So, tell me about the case that you, and you alone, solved Mr. Detective."

"I need to shower first, then I'm going to make passion-ate love to you. Then, when the sun rises, I'll tell you the story of my heroics."

He kisses her again, and heads to the bathroom, as she smiles, knowing he'll be asleep two minutes after his head hits the pillow.

CHAPTER 54

The next day, Brian, his captain, and the DA meet in her office. It's on the third floor of one of the older buildings in the city, but it has the feeling of power. The marble floors, high ceilings, and heavy wooden doors create an atmosphere of what Brian likes to think of as a real Hall of Justice. Even the steps are marble.

The police captain and Brian were well acquainted with the DA, Sheila Bryant. Because of that, they have a great deal of admiration for her. She is an attractive 54 year-old with a reputation that seems to frighten young defense lawyers. Her stature and controlled demeanor have fooled lawyers for 15 years, ever since she took over the position from her late boss. However, her staff loves her, and knows that she has their backs, even when they screw up a case. As she tells them, "You don't screw up, you don't learn." There are very few screw ups in her department. The two officers have given her a rundown on Edward Teller, and the story behind his desire for revenge. Brian has tried to keep his personal feelings out of the information he conveys, knowing that Sheila will use the facts, and produce her own emotions in the courtroom. He finishes by telling her that the police still have not captured the person who shot Edward Teller's son.

"Personally, that is none of my business," she says. "This is a homicide. This was premeditated. We have him confessing to six murders of young children in the most horrible way. Please give me cases like this every day, and I'll make the Baltimore police department look like Supermen." She never smiled, but Brian was happy she thought the work they had done was good, even exceptional.

He knew just how poorly the people of Baltimore felt about their police department. "I should have the grand jury indictment by the weekend. We will ask, and I'm sure I can persuade the judge, to forgo any type of bail that his lawyer will ask for. I'm also going to ask for the trial to be sequestered, so that the press doesn't give this madman any help. I want this to be clean and quick. The sooner he's found guilty on all counts, the better off we all are. I have a feeling that after I address the jury with the horrendous crimes he was responsible for, they'll ask me for a rope to hang him here in the courthouse. Thank you for your work, Brian. The captain tells me that most of it was your doing. A hell of a job, really. I wish to God I had more clean cases like this one," holding the paperwork that Brian had brought to her.

They shook hands, and Sam and Brian left.

CHAPTER 55

By the time Edward Teller reached the police station his lawyer, Ronald Casey, was waiting for him. Casey is known in the courts as "Killer Casey" because of all the murderers he defended over his 35-year career. He has been successful by not just getting some of them off, but getting others shorter sentences, when everyone knew they deserved to spend the rest of their lives doing hard labor for the crimes they had committed. Casey is tall, standing above 6'3" and weighing in at around 230. He works out religiously every day, and lays in his tanning machine after each workout. He has a full head of salt and pepper hair, which he wears shoulder length, and is what one might call unruly. He dresses in Armani, and wears $1000 loafers he bought in Italy, made just for his large size 13 feet. Being single adds to the mystique he presents, especially to women jurists, who seem to always want to please him. His deep baritone voice often brings people to attention, who were fast asleep in the back of the courtroom. He loves big trials and, when

Edward had called him and told him what he had done and why, he immediately decided he was on board.

Casey enters the front door of the station. The officer sitting behind the front desk looks up, recognizes him, and smiles.

"So, what can I do for you, counselor?"

"Good morning, Aaron. I'm here to meet with my client, Ed Teller. I understand he was brought in earlier, and I need to speak with him."

"You know the rules. He has to go through the normal procedure before we can let you in. It shouldn't take more than a couple hours, if you want to wait."

"I have a meeting outside with the press. I'll be back shortly."

He then walks to the front of the station and meets with several news reporters he had called. He doesn't climb up any stairs, but carefully lowers his voice, to get their attention, and says, "We keep hearing about the poor black kids killed by the police. It's awful. However, what happens when one of those kids shoots down an innocent 10 year-old white boy in the middle of the day, in broad daylight, and the shooter is never apprehended. Most of the time this police department doesn't even pursue the criminal. Why is that? Why does the public, black and white, come out to protest the killing of a young black child but the white child doesn't even get noticed? Well, let me tell you. You will hear shortly about a man who decided to take the issue into his own hands, and get revenge on those who killed his young son. A boy innocently walking on the streets of downtown

Baltimore. Murdered. And worse. To this day, no one has been arrested. And by the way, the murder of his son was over two years ago. To make this more outrageous, the boy's mother was with him when he was shot and has been institutionalized since then. Do we call this just one murder when two people lose their lives? Stay tuned, ladies and gentlemen."

He walks away, leaving them on their phones.

CHAPTER 56

Before Brian left for his meeting with the DA, he and Sally wake up to see *The Baltimore Sun* headline saying, "Child Killer Captured." It was the first time the two of them had a chance to have coffee together in days, and Sally wanted to hear what was going on with this killer. She understood Brian's need to keep much of the information secret until after the trial, but she also knew his need to discuss these cases with her, so that he could get them off his chest.

After reading the headlines, Brian says, "Well, here we go."

Sally responds, "You've been there before and, I'm afraid, you'll be there again. So, why don't you tell me just what's going on?"

Giving Sally the abbreviated version of what has taken place regarding this case so far, including his meetings with the various gang leaders, and all the help Terry has been in communicating with the families of the gangs, he finally describes his face-to-face meeting with Ed Teller.

"I'll tell you Sally, this old guy did some awful things and, while I sat there trying to be objective, I found myself hurting for him. He doesn't care if they send him to prison or not. He wanted to make a statement. As he sees it, he really only wanted revenge for what the gangs and the system had done to him and his family. I just have to remember, as Sheila Bryant says, 'He killed 6 innocent little children in cold blood.' I won't, and hope the jury doesn't, give him a pass on that."

As he spoke, Sally's thoughts went back to years ago when she and Brian first dated. Sally had married a young police officer, who she fell in love with the first time he kissed her. Brian was shy when they first met and dated. He never held her hand in public, although he did when they went to a movie. She remembers the first time he put his arm around her in the theater, and how she had quickly encouraged him by placing her head on his shoulder. When he drove her home that night, as he put the car in park, he turned to her, took her face in his hands, and softly kissed her. She remembers responding, and kissing him more deeply. They kissed like that for what seemed hours, but was only minutes, before he moved away and said, "Your mother is probably watching from the upstairs window, as she always does when I bring you home."

Sally acknowledged that what he said was probably true but, instead of opening the door and leaving, she moved closer to him, and kissed him again. "It was a wonderful night Brian, thank you." Hoping he would respond to her by saying let's do it again tomorrow. He didn't, and she was up half the night worrying if she had done something wrong. Her junior college classes began early, so she left the house and headed for the bus stop. As she approached the bus stop, she saw his car waiting. She walked over to the passenger side and got in. "What are you doing here?" she asked.

He turned around in the seat and faced her. "I've been here all night. I knew where and when you caught the bus for school, and I wanted to talk to you. I should have said this last night, but the words just didn't come to me. As you know already, I'm not the most articulate person in the world."

She smiled now, understanding just how difficult a time he was having, and leaned over to him and took one of his hands in hers. "Whatever you want to say, Brian, I'm here, I'm not going anywhere."

"Sally, I'm crazy about you. I believe you like me as well. It's just that I'm not ready to get married or anything like that, do you understand?"

"Why are you concerned about this, Brian?"

"Well, it's just that we've only been seeing each other for a short time, and we both want this to continue, and you're still in school, and Jesus, I'm going nuts thinking about you all the time...and getting married is such a big deal. I'm not being clear, am I?"

"Brian, stop and catch your breath," she said, still holding his hand. "I never mentioned getting married now. You're right, I'd rather wait until I graduate and get my accounting degree. I feel the same about you as you say you do about me. I think I fell in love with you the first time you kissed me. I'm not in a rush for a ring but, I do not want to lose you. I want to see you every day. I want your arms around me all the time, and I hunger for your kisses. Is that what you want to hear?"

"It's the girl I've fallen in love with talking. You've taken a massive boulder off my back. I've been so worried, that I was either too fast or too slow, and that you were getting tired of me. I'm not the kind of guy who wants every girl to jump into bed with him. I have had very little experience with women, as I'm sure you already surmised. You're going to have to bear with me if we want this to work. I need you to tell me when I'm too fast, or too slow. I never, and I mean never, want to hurt you in any way. I've never been with anyone with whom I felt comfortable to discuss my inner-most feelings. After I'm with you, I feel grown-up. Now that's strange, isn't it?"

"I think I know what you mean. It feels as if we belong together already, like we're an old married couple."

"That's exactly what I meant. You're amazing. He leans over, gently kisses her, and says, "How about I drive you to class, then I need to get home and change clothes for work. This is going to be a very long day."

CHAPTER 57

First, Sheila presents her case to the Grand Jury, and gets an indictment. Sheila Bryant is not happy with but, understands the slow process, and is pleased that no bail has been granted, so Teller is going to stay locked up until the trial. She tries to stay focused and, instead of worrying, she works closely with her staff putting the finishing touches on the case. From every angle she looks at the case. It seems absolutely air tight. However, she's been a DA long enough to know there is no such thing as air tight. She has watched TV, and listened to the radio, and seen enough newspaper copy about this "poor man who lost his family," over the last three months to make her gag. She knows this is all Ron Casey's doing, but also knows that, once in the courtroom she will prevail. His confession to two officers on tape, in his own home, under no duress, was enough to convict him. She wants him locked away forever, period.

The trial will begin right after the New Year, so that the jury pool will not be hindered by the holiday season. She has asked for, and been granted, sequestration of the jurors by the judge. This has angered Casey since he knows that, although you ask the jurors not to read the papers or watch TV, they do anyway, and are frequently persuaded not by the facts of the case, but by the rhetoric they consumed at home.

Her list of witnesses is excellent; all professionals. She had decided not to include the families of the deceased children, since having emotional outcries never won cases. The other problem with having the parents of the children on the stand was that they were all gang families involved in drugs, and she knew Casey would tear them apart. She might use the mothers, when it came to sentencing. Lots of tears never hurt when it came to swaying a judge about time to be served.

The judge assigned to the case is Paul Henderson, a strictly by the book, no nonsense scholar, whom Sheila likes very much. She has an idea that he will not put up with some of the antics that Casey likes to throw at the jurors. Judge Henderson retired several years ago, and just recently returned after his wife of 30 years was killed in an automobile accident. She remembers him as an assistant DA who had a superb conviction rating. She also remembers wondering if he was married, since he never wore a wedding ring. She had considered asking him out, until she found out he was married.

The most compelling evidence Sheila has is the pictures from the basement of the house on Lake Drive. Those alone should be enough for a guilty verdict.

CHAPTER 58

———

Sue, who is now living with Bob Turner, gets an email from the Baltimore Press Association congratulating her for winning this year's Reporter of the Year award. She stares at it, looks around the press room for Bob and, not seeing him, prints a copy and walks over to Ralph's office.

"Have you seen Bob?"

"No, I think he's out on a follow-up interview with the fire department, regarding that mysterious death in the burned-out building uptown. Is there something I can help with?"

She drops the copy of the notice on his desk, and waits for him to read it.

"Congratulations! This is wonderful. I think you need to get in touch with Bob, don't you?"

She heads back to her desk, calls Bob's cell, and waits for an answer. After two rings, he says, "So, how's my favorite reporter?"

"Bob, I just received an email from the Baltimore Press

Association making me the recipient of this year's Reporter of the Year award."

"Amazing as it might seem, I'm not surprised. I sent copies of all your articles, regarding the six murdered kids, to a dozen reporters and editors around town. They must have read them. That's a miracle in itself. You know you deserve it, don't you? The series was spectacular and, I might add with pride, that I was the person who gave you your first break."

"But you are as responsible for the story as I was."

"True, but you followed up on it, and wrote the articles, while I ran around looking for more stories. No, this is yours and, tonight I'll open a nice bottle of champagne, and we'll go out and celebrate."

"Bob, I love you, but we're not going out anywhere tonight."

"Oh, Jesus, bring home lots of lotion."

CHAPTER 59

Terry and Monica's wedding was Baltimore's social event of the season. Every newspaper and TV channel reported something about it. Terry had never seen so many dignitaries in one place. There were even several tables devoted to young techies. The best part was getting into the limo afterwards, and heading for the airport.

The week in New York flew by. They saw several wonderful Broadway shows and missed several, having no strength to get out of bed. They ate themselves silly at 4-star restaurants and hot dog stands.

When they arrived home and opened their apartment door, the first thing they saw was a huge bouquet of flowers, in a beautiful vase, with a card hanging from it. Monica pulled the card off, expecting to see her parents' name but, was surprised to see "A wish for good health and long life from your 4 Baltimore buddies." Monica's eyes teared up, and Terry put his arm around her and said, "I think we picked the right partners, don't you?"

As they carried their luggage into the bedroom, Monica says, "I'm not sure if I'm happy to see tomorrow come or not. We've given ourselves some high hurdles to climb over with this project."

Terry puts his suitcase down, takes Monica's from her, drops it on the floor next to his and says, "Right now, Mrs. Stein, I don't think this is the time to worry about tomorrow. It's still today, and I want to spend it with my wife, not any partnership." He takes her in his arms and glides her over to the bed.

The next day, they are sitting at the kitchen table discussing the development plans. They're pushing the city to allow them to begin bulldozing the property, since the evidence had been accumulated, photos taken, and the police did not want crazies taking the house apart as souvenirs. Fortunately, the city wants to pass ownership over to the corporation as quickly as possible.

Monica explained to the group that, in all probability, it would take them a year to clear the property of the remnants of buildings that still remained, complete the architectural drawings, and get approvals from the city.

Sol had set up an account at the bank for their use, and Terry and Monica had met with the group to discuss plans as well as how each of them could help expedite the work ahead. There was total enthusiasm for what they all saw as a life-long commitment to what began as just an idea to make a couple dollars on the side.

By the time work was to begin, they hoped everyone would forget about what happened in the house on Lake

Drive. If they were able to get approval quickly, they would have the city come in and begin the process of upgrading all the sewage pipes. Sol proposed they use fiber optics underground, for all the wiring in the development, thus no overhead cables would be seen. He also suggested they get a professional landscape company to begin planting trees as soon as they could, so that by the time the entire neighborhood was completed, the trees would have some height, and enhance the value for everyone buying there. All these plans were being put together by the group, and each had taken on part of the responsibility for expediting the process.

They had hired several administrative assistants to help with the paperwork and record keeping. All those hired were from the inner city, at Monica's request. They were currently using Terry's offices but had decided, with Sol's approval, to take over an old building he owned that was very close to the project. It was large enough to expand as they began to build.

Although Terry was an integral part of the project, he put in many hours with Sol, going through the folders he had been given, educating himself on the vast holdings of their company. The financial size of the holdings that Sol had talked about originally, Terry saw was just a small part of portfolio of businesses.

What Terry enjoyed most was having long lunches with Sol, asking questions, and meeting numerous officers, partners, bankers, politicians, and friends of every size, shape, gender, and color. His admiration for Sol grew every day. He felt encouraged that Sol opened up to him about things that he said even Becky probably doesn't know about. The more confidences he shared with Terry, the more Terry worked harder to understand the nuances of the businesses, and his work. Terry did suggest to Sol that he let him hire an administrative assistant, to help him organize his work with Sol and the new development.

Sol liked the idea, and told him he did not need his permission to hire or fire anyone any longer. He trusted him to move forward and hire who he and the company needed for their future growth. He also suggested that if Terry felt he needed more help, he should look at the office space on the floor above him, which was larger and would accommodate the added personnel. All in all he and Monica were busy all the time. It was good in a way, since it took their minds off the trial.

CHAPTER 60

For Brian, everything was moving quickly. He was kept busy with the trial and chasing down the new influx of drugs in the downtown area. The DA had won her requests for no bail, and to have the jury sequestered, which meant Brian was able to spend his time thinking about the new problems in his precinct. Terry had kept him aware of the severe drug problems in the city. Several high school children had overdosed, and many others become seriously ill, when they had taken some kind of new synthetic drug that was rampant throughout the city. What Brian knew was, the gangs whose children were killed, had all prospered, and seemed to have a new respect for each other. There hadn't been a drive-by shooting since Teller was captured. This was a new concern for Brian. He increased his police cruiser patrols in many neighborhoods, and made sure that the officers on patrol had grown up in Baltimore, and still lived here. He knew that, since the children's disappearance, the serious crime rate in their neighborhoods had dropped 20%.

It meant, he hoped, that people felt they could walk their streets without as much fear. Drive-by shootings had all but ceased. He intended to keep it that way. If anything out of the ordinary happened, he told his officers he wanted them to call him directly on his cell.

At the same time, he was helping the DA put the finishing touches on her case. He had been in her office more times than for any case he had ever been involved with. The DA had questioned him so many times, he felt like *he* was on trial, and not Teller. He was anxious about the negative publicity the police was receiving in some parts of town, because of the constant appearances of Casey, but he tried to keep that from the rest of his officers. When things were going right, you did not want to throw any problems into the pot. However, he knew from experience, that any day the current peace could be broken.

The brightest part of his day was going over to see Bridget and her daughter, Sue Ellen. The two of them brought a smile to his face every time he saw them. For a long time, it was impossible to imagine Bridget married. Now, here she was with this gorgeous daughter, his grandchild. Sally had all but moved in with them. Nowadays when Brian came home for dinner, it was frozen food put together at the last minute, because she didn't get home until late. He didn't care, although he missed the great meals Sally cooked.

Sitting in his office, he was thinking about one of his favorite meals, when his cellphone rang. "Murphy."

"Heh, Lieutenant. Officer Barry Medford. Sorry to

bother you, but I thought you'd want to hear the latest news I just received here at the station."

"Tell me," Brian says, hoping it's good news for a change, but knowing it probably isn't.

"There was an armed robbery downtown. Two kids held up a jewelry store. Not a smart idea since, according to the report, the owner pulled out his own gun, shot and killed one of the two kids and the other he shot, and this is the best part, in the ass. The wounded kid is on the way to the hospital, and the morgue has the other one."

"Sort of all's well that ends well, I'd say," says Brian.

"But that's not the best part. Seems the gun they had was the same one that was used on the Good Humor shooting. How about that?"

Brian now understands why he got the call, and why the officer was so happy about the outcome.

"Great news. Has the DA been notified?"

"I believe so, but I'll double-check. By the way, the two kids are Jack Hubbard's younger brothers, Juan and Mateo."

"Jesus, will they never learn? Thanks for the call, I appreciate it. Keep me posted on what else the DA finds."

Brian then calls Jack Hubbard at home. A youngster answers, "What?"

Brian says, "This is Lt.. Murphy. I need to speak to Jack, now."

"He ain't here."

"Find him, and have him call me right away. It's very important, do you understand?"

"I understand, man. What you think?"

"I just need to talk to him now, so have him call me on my cell. He has the number," and he hangs up.

Ten minutes later, almost on the dot, his cellphone rings. "Murphy."

"Jack Hubbard."

"Jack, I'm calling to extend to you and your family my condolences. I'm truly sorry for what happened to your brother."

"Fucking fools, that's what they were. They knew better. What the hell they going and robbing that store for? Assholes."

"Jack, one of them is still in the hospital. He's hurting in more ways than one. He'll probably go through juvenile court, because of his age, and he wasn't the one carrying, from what I've been told. He's going to need your help. You can be a good or a bad influence on him right now, it's up to you. I just want you to know that if you need my help, give me a call. Okay?"

"I hear you, and thanks."

CHAPTER 61

The only people that seem delighted to begin a criminal trial are the judge, the prosecutor, and the defense lawyers. The judge, because he or she has the opportunity to show the power that the state has given them to judge, based on his or her experience and knowledge. It is an honor, most of the time, to be a judge. Other times, when the judge has been elected, they have the problem of making sure their judgment coincides with the popular view.

Once the trial has begun, the judge is the person everyone must cater to. The prosecutor is eager to throw someone in jail, and usually only prosecutes when they believe they can win a case. They usually do, although most are settled before the trial begins. Once we get to the defense lawyer, it gets complicated. Most are assigned cases by the court because the defendant can't afford a lawyer. The majority of these cases are going to be settled before they enter the courtroom. The few that defend clients that can afford their fees are also divided. There are the defense lawyers who truly believe in the law, and want to see justice done. They are wonderful lawyers, often living on the edge of poverty, but the happiest lawyers when they win a case. They work out payments with their clients, and celebrate victories as hard as the people they defend.

The category "Killer Casey" fell into was none of the above. He had, over the years, made his reputation by handling cases no one else would touch. Along with those cases, he received more than enough publicity to have defendants line up to get him as their attorney. He lived well, in a large home on the eastern shore of Maryland, with a 48' sailboat, and a 500 series Mercedes. His bank account and investments meant he could afford to take any case he wanted. Of course, that didn't stop him from asking for a half million dollars up front from Edward Teller, to handle the case, even though he knew the only thing he could do for Ed was give him the publicity and the stage to present his case to the public. He was there as an expeditor. He wanted Ed to have his day in court, but he also wanted Ed to receive the public's empathy before the trial began. That's what Ed wanted, and Casey worked every news agency he knew to make sure the public was hearing Ed's story before the trial began and the DA threw all "the facts" at everyone. He always thought that facts confuse the issue, and believed he could make most of the facts DAs presented look less than absolute, once he worked the jury.

As Sheila sat in the courtroom, looking at the list of potential jurors for Teller's trial, she began to cross out all the men she felt would empathize with him. Then she looked for any older people who she discounted. The people she liked for the jury were women who might have small children. They were the diamonds she wanted. Across from her, where Casey would sit, the table was empty. No one had seen him for days, and the judge would be calling in the pool any minute. As the judge walked into the court, everyone stood up and, out of the corner of her eye, Sheila saw Ronald Casey come strolling up the aisle as if he was going in to see a movie. He sat down when everyone else did. He sat just across from Sheila, looked over at her, smiled and waved.

"Goddamn him," she thought. "What a smug son of a bitch he can be. He knows he has no chance to win this case. His client is guilty as hell, and even the people who have sympathy for Teller know that. He hasn't even given a list to us, or the judge, of witnesses he would be calling in support of his client. If I was his client, I'd be really pissed off at him. Let him wave at me."

The judge asked the officer in the back of the room to call in the first fifty prospective jurors. They marched in, looked around at who was there and, just as Sheila had feared, all the women seemed to look at Casey in his grey pin-striped suit, blue shirt, and bright red silk tie. Her prediction, however, of a conflict with Casey over the seating of the jurors was confusingly wrong. This bothered her, since he made no comment at all during the picking of the jurors.

Sheila was elated that she got all the women on the jury she wanted. Even the judge asked Casey if he was participating in the selection of the jury. Casey stood and addressed the judge saying, "Our illustrious DA is picking the same jurors I would pick, your honor. I have no problem with her selections," and he sat down.

It took less than two hours to find the 12 jurors and 2 alternates. Before the selection began, the jurors were told by the judge that they would be sequestered during the trial. The jurors who had been chosen knew that they would be away from home for an extended period of time. Sheila knew that her list of witnesses would take at least a week, and the fact that Casey didn't have a list meant to her that he would try his best to use her witnesses to prove his case.

She and her staff had spent months with the witnesses, going over and over just what to expect from Casey but, she knew from experience, he would throw something into the mix to confuse even the best witness. Well, we'll see what he does tomorrow.

CHAPTER 62

It's fair to say that most defendants are nervous and full of fear just before they face a jury, especially in a murder case. They are counseled by their lawyer just how to act. "Don't sit stoically. Face the jury. Try not to let your emotions show when you hear something that you know is untrue. People lie, witnesses lie, but don't you lie." The counseling goes on until the day of the trial, sometimes during.

Edward Teller was not a typical defendant. When he was marched into the courtroom on the first day, with every seat filled and TV and newspaper reporters watching, he was not in the least bit nervous. He knew the outcome and, at his age, he understood he would probably spend the rest of his life in prison. He had been in his own prison since his son died, and he had to place his wife in an asylum. There was nothing more that society could do to him. His goal during this trial was to get his message across. He felt confident that would happen. He looked around the room, then at the prosecutor's table, and then averted his eyes long enough to find his lawyer, and then back to the prosecutor. He didn't smile, but looked directly at her as if to say, "It's my turn."

Sheila looked back at him like he was dirt, and smiled. She was not afraid of him, or his lawyer, and was prepared to skewer him to the wall, if necessary.

The judge asked the two lawyers if they were ready, and the trial began. Sheila began with her opening, smoothing her skirt and buttoning her jacket as she got up, and approached the jury. These were mostly women, mostly black and Hispanic, and most had small children at home with parents or sitters. She knew their burden. She had raised two children on her own, after her husband had been killed by a drunk driver, starting when they were just 2 and 4 years old. The hardship that she put her parents through, to raise those two while she finished college and law school, still sat on her conscience, although they insisted their love for her and their grandchildren overshadowed any burden they felt. These were her women. The two men sitting in the box were important but, she spoke to the women, knowing that their insight would carry the day, once they had heard the whole case.

"Ladies and gentlemen. First, thank you for your time to be here today. As a mother of two, I understand and appreciate the burden that jury service puts on you, so I will keep my opening statement short."

Turning around, and pointing at Teller, she says, "Edward Teller is a cold-blooded murderer."

She turns back to them and says, "Even worse, he is a cold-blooded murderer who planned and executed the killing of six young children. You will hear how he lost his own child to gun violence years ago but, even he will admit, no one knows for sure who shot his son. It could have been anyone. No one witnessed the shooting, except his wife, and you will hear from the defense how this poor woman has, from the moment of the death of her son, lost her mind. She has been institutionalized since then, unable to communicate anything at all. A tragedy. Our hearts go out to him for his loss."

She pauses, letting the jury absorb the idea that Teller's case of 'poor me' was what they were likely to hear. After a few seconds, she looks at them, and raises her voice just enough to get their attention, saying, "However, that is not the murder case we are trying today. No, that one is still unsolved and, in truth, might never be solved. It has no bearing on the murder of these children. This murderer decided to take out his sick revenge on innocent children, rather than pursue justice the way all the rest of society does. He, and he alone, decided who was to be found guilty of the murder of his child. He, and he alone, planned and conducted this unbelievable series of murders. Did he think that would bring his son back, or make his wife well? Of course not. Did he ever think about the parents of these children he murdered, and what their pain would be? Of course not. What he wanted was, and these are his own words, "revenge". She made sure that the last word was emphasized. "Revenge murders of small children, whose parents and families he could not have possibly known were a part of the killing of his own son."

"I will show you how he put this plan together, traveling into Pennsylvania to purchase the old ice cream truck. How he went to the city for a permit, signed contracts for the equipment and ice cream, purchased the plastic to kill and wrap these children in, broke into a deserted house on Lake Drive, and prepared it to be his hiding place for those poor, dead children. We will show you how he murdered them by putting heavy plastic bags over their little heads. In all the years I have been in the District Attorney's office, this is this worst crime I have ever experienced."

The weeping of some of the parents of the children could be heard loud enough so that several jurors turned to see who was crying. Again, Sheila turns to face the defendant and, again, points to Teller. "He did it. He admits on tape he did it. He admits to placing the plastic over their heads. He admits to watching them as the air ran out, and they eventually died. He was not coerced into making the recording for the police, but decided to tell them that he did it. This is an open and shut case. The only thing I'm sorry about is that the state of Maryland doesn't have the death penalty any longer, because that's what he deserves. Please see to it he never gets the opportunity to commit more of these crimes. Find him guilty and throw away the key. Thank you."

She walked back to her table, sat down, and took a deep breath. Her assistant DA leaned over and said, "Well done."

CHAPTER 63

The judge looked over at Casey and said, "Are you ready, Mr. Casey?"

Casey stood up and, looking over at the jury and then back to the judge, says "If your honor pleases, I will hold my opening statement until after the prosecution has completed their case."

The judge looks back at Sheila, who is still worried about some crazy tactic that Casey might throw their way, and hears the judge ask, "Is the prosecution ready?"

"Yes, your Honor."

Sheila stands up and places a number of folders on the table in front of her, one for each of her witnesses, and says, "Your honor, I'd like to call my first witness."

Over the next week Sheila presents her case, step-by-step, constantly reminding the jury that everything about this man's case was premeditated. Nothing was left to chance. Each witness confirmed what Sheila was stating. What surprised Sheila was that Casey did not rebut or deny any of the testimony. He sat there with Teller, quietly listening to everything being said, as if they were enjoying a movie. The judge continuously asked Casey if he wished to address the witness and Casey stood, looked at the witnesses, then said quietly, "No, your honor."

When Sheila brought out the pictures of the dead children, lying side by side with the plastic bags still tied over their heads, half the women in the jury began to cry.

Sheila had placed the enlarged pictures on an easel, rather than have the jurors pass them around. She did this because she wanted to leave the picture up as long as possible for each of the jurors to absorb the actual sight of the crime.

She knew from experience that these jurors, including the men, would have nightmares about what they were seeing but, that was what would motivate them when it came time to convict. These pictures proved to them that this was not some abstract theory of murder; this was the real thing.

Again, the judge looked over at Casey to see if he wanted time to respond or object but, seeing him look his way, Casey simply waved his hand to say it's okay.

The last witness for the prosecution was Lt. Brian Murphy, who had led the investigation and had taped Teller's full confession. He was a key witness, although Sheila felt her case had already been won. She had no idea what Casey was up to, but wanted to close her case with as solid a witness as possible.

Brian sat in the witness chair not for the first time. He knew what the prosecution was going to ask him, and had come prepared with copies of all the notes and reports he had submitted. He knew his memory was not as sharp as it used to be, and he did not want the defense lawyer to throw him a curve that he could not hit out of the ballpark.

Sheila walked him through the case from day one, when he approached Terry Stein, who had already been on the stand as a witness. He opened his folder and read off, almost day-by-day, what he and the Baltimore police force had done to find and capture the defendant.

"Lieutenant, you did not capture him as much as he turned himself in. Isn't that correct?"

Brian looked up at her and answered, "That's correct. He called in to the station and confessed, and then gave his name and address so someone could come out to his home and hear his whole story."

"In other words, he insisted that he had murdered these children, and wanted the police to hear his confession, correct?"

"Yes, that's correct."

"And did you go out to his home in Stevenson and tape his confession?"

"I did, with detective Sam Delgado of the Stevenson police department. It was his tape recorder we used to record the confession."

Sheila turns to the jurors and says, "I'm going to play this recording for you. However," turning to the judge, "It is over an hour long, your honor. Can we break for lunch, and listen to the entire tape after we return?"

The judge looks at his watch and says, "Court is adjourned until 1:30."

Brian approaches Sheila before she leaves for lunch, and asks, "You'll need me here after lunch, I assume?"

"Of course. You're my key witness."

Brian walks outside the courtroom, and spots Terry speaking with a parent of one of the deceased children. He waits until Terry's free, and walks over and asks, "She okay?"

"Yes, but seeing those pictures would turn anyone's stomach. You were very good up there, by the way."

"Thanks, but I've been there before, and it never gets easy. I'm heading out for a quick bite, can you join me?"

"That's a good idea. I forget to eat sometimes when I'm busy, and it really pisses Monica off. She takes care of me better than my own mother did."

"Well, she knows she married a big baby," answers Brian.

They laugh, and leave the courthouse.

CHAPTER 64

Back in the courtroom, Brian looked around for Sheila or one of her assistant DAs. She finally arrives and says, "You'll be the first one we call, so stick around."

Brian answers, "I'm not going anywhere."

Once court resumes, and Brian was back in the witness stand, Sheila had the tape recorder hooked up to a speaker to make it easier for everyone to hear. Then, she told the judge she was ready. He suggests she proceed, so she turned to the jury again and said, "Ladies and gentlemen, this is a difficult tape to listen to, but it is very important for you to hear the defendant acknowledge that he had killed all these children. Again, you will recognize the voice of Edward Teller, who is describing what occurred. If at any time you do not understand what is said, or need to ask a question, please raise your hand and I will stop the tape. Lt. Murphy is here to answer any questions you might have. Thank you for your continued attention."

As the tape rolled, the voice of the sergeant was heard

describing the situation, who he was interviewing, and stating that this was entirely voluntary by the defendant. Then, for what seemed hours, Edward Teller spoke. As he spoke, Brian noticed that the tape was having the same effect on the jury that it had on Sam and him. The first part of the taped interview, when Ed Teller had expressed his pain, about the loss of his son and his wife being institutionalized, had them looking sad. Then as it continued to play, the rest had them looking angry, especially when he described the capture and murder of the children. Once the tape was finished, and the speaker was placed back behind the DA's table, Sheila approached the jury and asked, "Are there any questions?" The jury looked around at each other, saw no one's hand go up, and looked back at Sheila.

She turned back to Brian and said, "No more questions, Lieutenant."

"Hold it," exclaimed Casey. "I have a few questions I'd like to ask."

Sheila, startled by Casey's outburst, raised her hands and walked back to her table.

Casey was granted his turn for questioning from the judge, and walked around to the front of the table. "Lt. Murphy, from all indications you were intimately involved with this case from the start. You and the officers from your station spent quite a bit of overtime investigating the missing children. Is that correct?"

"Yes," said Brian, keeping his answer short and to the point.

Casey, not fazed by the short answer continued, "I

understand, you've been an officer in the Baltimore police department for over 30 years. True?"

Again, Brian answered "Yes."

"Can you tell me off-hand, how many drive-by killings occurred during those years? Now, I'll not hold you to an exact number, but can you give me an idea?"

"Off-hand, I don't believe I can."

"Well, let me refresh your memory." Casey pulled out a small sheet of paper from his jacket and read the information written on it. "From what I have discovered from my poor computer, there have been an average of 350 murders each year in Baltimore, just in the last five years. During that same five-year period there have been four or five drive-by killings in the city each year on average. Would you say that's a fair number, Lieutenant?"

"If you say so."

"Oh, it's not me saying so, it's my computer. It also tells me that there have been no arrests for any of those crimes. Can you believe that? That's between 20 or 25 people in your city that have been murdered on the streets, and not one arrest."

Sheila finally jumped up, "I object, your honor. If Mr. Casey wants to take the Lieutenant through these questions, he should show some relevance. We are trying his client for the murder of six children. Mr. Casey should be told to stop the rhetoric and stay on point. The Lieutenant has more important business to attend to than listen to this nonsense."

"Your honor," Casey says, now looking at the jury and

not the judge, "I'm just trying to show this fine jury that our police force seems to take special care of the inner city children, and often times forgets about the rest of us."

Again Sheila jumped up and yells, "Your Honor, that's nothing less than bigotry he's spewing here in your court. I, for one, protest."

The judge banged his gavel, "Enough, Mr. Casey. We get your point. If you have nothing else to ask the Lt., please sit down."

"Just a couple more questions, your Honor. Would you say that having a mass murderer, as our illustrious District Attorney has classified Mr. Teller, call and give the police his location somewhat unusual?"

"Very," answers Brian.

"Would you say that bringing you into his home and volunteering to confess the crimes he committed was somewhat unusual?"

Brian doesn't know where the questions are going, but keeps the answers simple, "Yes."

"It was in your precinct where Randolph Teller, the 10 year-old son of my client, was murdered one afternoon on one of the busiest business streets in Baltimore. Is that not so?"

Again, "Yes."

"Do you recall the murder?"

Brian pulls out a sheet of paper from his folder and reads back to Casey the date, time, and location of the crime.

"So there we have it. Does your *sheet*," and Casey emphasizes the word 'sheet', "also tell you how many men you assigned to follow up on this murder of an innocent child?"

Again, Brian looks at the sheet and answers, "Two detectives were assigned to the case."

Pushing his point, Casey asks, "Does your sheet also tell you just how long that investigation took?"

Brian looks down at his notes, and then back up to Casey, and says, "Off and on for several weeks."

"Were there ever any suspects brought in or questioned?"

Again looking at his notes he responds, "No suspects, but over a dozen businesses questioned along with the people who might have witnessed the shooting."

"And then, I gather, like poor little Randolph, the file was buried, am I correct?"

"Objection, your honor," exclaims Sheila.

"Noted," says the judge looking over to Casey, who waves his hand to acknowledge the judge's reprimand.

"One last question. After you heard Mr. Teller's confession with Sergeant Delgado, do you remember what you said to him before he took my client away?"

Brian does remember and knows he needs to tell the truth because Casey has probably already gotten the answer from Delgado. So he answers, "Yes."

"Can you tell the jury what you said?"

"I can only paraphrase it, because I don't remember the exact words, but I believe I told him that I felt sorry for Mr. Teller's loss of both his son and wife."

Casey looks over to the jury, smiles and says, "Thank

you Lt. Murphy for your candor and honesty. That's all I have, your honor."

Casey, satisfied that the jurors had heard the witness's answer, sits down.

The judge turns to Sheila and asks her if she has any more questions for Lt. Murphy. She gets up from her seat, calmly walks around the table, putting questions together that she needed to ask, to get Murphy off the hot seat.

"The defense has tried to show that the Baltimore police department shows favor when it comes to arresting people for crimes. He suggests that when white people have a crime committed against them, the police look the other way. Have you ever heard of such nonsense?"

Now Brian had something to say. "If the defense lawyer had completed his research on his old computer, he would have found that our Maryland prisons are occupied far more by people of color than white. However, we arrest almost as many white people for crimes as people of color. The statistics show that unlike most people of color, the white people coming into the system bring in with them lawyers just like Mr. Casey." Even some of the jury smiled at that.

Sheila wants to end on this point and says to the judge, "We rest our case, your honor."

CHAPTER 65

The judge looked over at Ron Casey and says, after looking at his watch, "It's late, Mr. Casey. Can we begin your case tomorrow?"

Casey stands and, facing the judge, says, "Thank you, your honor. I believe tomorrow morning will be fine."

All the reporters move quickly to the doors after the jury leaves for their hotel rooms. The reporters are excited about the information they have written during the day, to either present it to their editors, or broadcast live on TV or radio. The jurors look exhausted as they moved slowly out to the bus.

Brian again sought Sheila out, before she disappeared out the front door. He touched her shoulder and said, "So, did we do okay?"

"Brian, I could not have done it without your testimony. Thank you again. Hopefully, all your good work will get us the conviction. I won't need you any longer on this case, so good luck. I'm afraid we'll be seeing each other again," she laughed.

"I think I'll be here in the morning to hear Edward's testimony, if he takes the stand."

"He's the only person listed by Casey, so I feel certain we will see him tomorrow."

Ed Teller sat in the holding cell finishing his dinner. Surprisingly, he had gained 10 pounds since his incarceration. He could not get enough food, and constantly asked for more. He no longer felt stressed, and slept like a baby on the rigid cot in his cell. He felt in control, for the first time since his son was murdered, and knew the ending to the story no matter how well he did tomorrow. That was fine with him. He was an old man willing to spend the rest of his life in prison for what he did. He had exacted his revenge, that could not be taken away from him. Casey had done the job he had paid him to do. It took the rest of his savings to get him to do it, but he knew he wouldn't need the money any longer, and didn't have anyone to leave the money to. Casey had spent some of the money he received to buy new outfits for Ed, so that as he walked into the courtroom each day, he looked like a businessman and not some crazy killer. He was ready for the last phase of this trial and knew he would sleep well tonight.

CHAPTER 66

Trials can be long and boring, but this one didn't fit that description. Because Casey had passed on all the DA's witnesses, other than Brian Murphy, the trial moved quickly. The jurors certainly didn't feel the trial was boring. Although, a number of them were acknowledging the pain and stress they felt listening to the DA describe the murders, and seeing the pictures of the dead children.

The courtroom was crowded, as usual. There was obvious tension in the room, with people talking loudly to one another, especially the family members of the children who had been murdered. They would hear this evil man for the first time. The police department had added several extra police, as security, and no one was allowed into the courtroom without being searched and going through a metal detector. Sheila and her assistant DAs were there early, trying to anticipate what they might hear in the testimony that Edward Teller would give.

After the judge entered and was seated, he called the court to order, and then asked Casey to present his defense.

"Your honor, I will take this time to make my opening statement." The judge acknowledged him and asked him to continue.

Ron Casey stood his full height and looked at the jury. He knew they were waiting for him to do something. He had passed on all the prosecutor's witnesses, and now they would expect him to bring his lineup up to the witness stand. Instead, he spoke to them quietly and said, "Ladies and gentlemen, you have heard the illustrious District Attorney present her case, and heard the tape with Mr. Teller's confession. Let me remind you that the trial is not over. You've heard one side only. Quite often we are persuaded by an issue, not realizing that we had focused on the one side we agree with, never giving the option a thought. It reminds me of a story used by my university professor. The course was statistics and the class was full. He stood in front of the class and asked just one question, after presenting his idea, which was, "If we were outside a movie theater, and 30% of the people who passed us raved about the movie, how many of us would rush over to buy tickets?" Just about the entire class raised their hands. After they had dropped their hands the professor said, "How amazing that you would jump at the 30% opinion without knowing what the other 70% thought. Possibly 70% thought it was crap."

At that, the jury understood, and most smiled at what he was saying. "The court has asked you to keep an open mind. I understand that part of what the District Attorney

said and showed you would tilt your opinion, even unknow-
ingly, to think that Mr. Teller is a monster. I want you to
hear the other side of the story, the 70%. In other words,
I'm asking you to give Mr. Teller the benefit of the doubt,
because he is the 70%."

He turned and called Edward Teller to the stand. There
was a noticeable murmur, which the judge quickly quieted.
"I will not have any interruptions in this court."

Edward Teller slowly, but deliberately, walked up to the
stand and was sworn in. Casey stood in front of his table
and said to Ed, "I'm sure you are tired of hearing all the negative things said about you, so I would like you to tell the
jury the why. Why did you do this? Why did you choose
these little children? Why did you choose the children of
gang leaders in Baltimore? Why not just hurt them or beat
them? Why kill them? Mr. Teller, the jury needs to know
what was in your mind. They need to know that this was
not an act of some maniac. So, Mr. Teller, would you please
speak to these jurors and tell them your view of the 70%?"

CHAPTER 67

Ed turned toward the jurors and took a deep breath. "I was born and raised in Baltimore. I worked my way through college, and continued to earn my CPA qualification at the University of Maryland. I began work at an accounting firm and worked my way up to be a Senior Vice President. The record shows that I had never even had a parking ticket in all the years leading up to the death of my son. I met my wife who, as you have heard, is now cared for in an asylum, because of the death of our son. But, I'm getting ahead of myself. We were not youngsters when we married. We loved each other but assumed, because of our ages, we would never have children. You can imagine how happy we both were when Sharon found out she was pregnant. Those 9 months were difficult for her. Not just the pregnancy, but the fear that at her age, she might have a child that was not perfect, kept her on edge. When our son Randy was born, as perfect as any child ever born, we both felt God had given us the biggest gift any one could receive."

The DA is about to object and then decides not to. She thinks, "Let him get his story out to the jury. He has already admitted killing those children and I have it on tape."

He stopped to take out his handkerchief and wipe his eyes. "Excuse me," he muttered and then he continued, "Because I had the ability to pay for the best schools, Randy went to a preschool out in Stevenson, which cost almost what it cost me to go to college. This continued when he entered a private elementary school. There was nothing too good for him and, instead of being a spoiled kid, he was the most adoring little boy you could imagine. His IQ was exceptional, and he made many friends. Sharon never let him go to bed without hugging her, so she could tell him how much he was loved.

"The ten years we spent with him were the happiest that Sharon and I had ever experienced. It seemed to Sharon and me that he was learning faster than we could teach him. I'm probably rambling about my son but, since Sharon and I understood that Randy was the only child we would ever have, he became the center of our lives. I'm sure many of you know the feeling. That delight when you arrive home, and there he is smiling and running into your arms. Watching your son play ball on weekends, or going with him to the movie and watching his eyes as if he were the first person to ever see the special animation on the screen."

"Look," he said, "I used to get up at 2 a.m., when he cried as an infant, so I could hold him and give him his bottle. He would look up at me and, within minutes close his eyes and sleep. After he died, for the first time since he was born, I began to feel old. That boy kept me and Sharon young. He brought vitality to our lives. He gave each day meaning and never asked us for any more than to be loved. And we loved him. We truly loved our son." Again he wiped his eyes and took another breath.

The judge asked, "Would you like a recess, Mr. Teller?"

"I'm okay. I'd like to finish my story." He turned back to the jurors and continued.

"The day Sharon brought Randy downtown to meet me for dinner, she had every right to believe she and Randy would be fine. After all, this is a civilized city with safe streets, right?" He paused. "Not right. Usually you read or hear about the killings in parts of the city where large populations of minorities live. Usually you hear about gangs shooting each other. What you never hear in Baltimore, as I found out the hard way, is how the police department solves these drive-by killings. This is precisely what I encountered for over a year after my son's murder, at the hands of one of these gangs during a drive-by fight. And, to add insult to injury, the police would say to me, "How do you know that they were gang members, it could have been anyone?"

"Are they kidding? Do they believe the public are a bunch of idiots? That is the attitude I was faced with almost every day when I called the police, or went to the police station to see what they had discovered about the killers of my son. For the first time, I understood that being a victim in Baltimore, and seeking justice, depended on whether or not the press and the public began to shout and get involved. They react to the killing of a black or Hispanic child because the families come out and yell. The churches come out and yell, and even some of the white churches come out and yell. However, can any of you think of a time when a white child was murdered on the streets by a drive-by shooter, that you saw it reported on the front page of any newspaper? I certainly can't."

Looking out at the press corps, Ed repeats his statement, "Have any of you press people ever seen a headline about a white child being shot down in the streets of Baltimore? Do you even know if that happens? Was my son the first and only white kid killed by gang shootings? I understand these questions are rhetorical, but they are the questions that I kept asking myself over and over again, as I buried my son and institutionalized my wife. These are the kind of questions that haunted me. Not just why me, but why, period? Why do we, as a civilized society, allow this to happen? Are we blind to what is going on in our city, and cities across the country, or are we afraid to look at the reality of what is going on? Let me say here, to all of you in the jury and in the press, I am not, and have never been bigoted. I did not choose to take the lives of those children because they were black or Hispanic. I took them to prove to the world that losing a child, no matter what their color or ethnic background, will create a massive hole in that family that all the world's sympathy will not fill. The families of the children I killed are no more or no less in pain than I have been. However, now they understand that, because they allowed their families to go around shooting each other, because they allowed young preteens to use and sell the drugs, because they condone the use of guns in their neighborhood without telling the authorities where they are and who's using them, then they are as responsible for the death of their children as I am. Their child could have been my child. Their loss is my loss, but their participation in the on-going crime of this city is theirs, and theirs alone. I want them to feel the pain. I want them to think about what their son or daughter might have been if they had lived. This was an act of revenge on my part. It also was an act of love for the family I lost. I am, as I said earlier, an old man. I expect I will live the rest of my life in prison. I have no illusions about that. I instructed my attorney not to question the District Attorney's witnesses, because I know they are good and honest people, and I did not want to denigrate their testimony in any way. What I wanted to tell this court, and the public, is that there is a cause and effect to life. You cannot throw a stone in the water without expecting some ripples, and you can't take people's lives without possibly forfeiting your own. My wife and son's lives were forfeited. I intended to forfeit the lives of other families for revenge. I have no apology to give to anyone. Personally, I doubt if my actions will have any effect on the crime in this city, or any other city. It won't be because I didn't warn you."

He turned and faced the judge and said, "Thank you, your honor, for the opportunity to tell my story. I hope I wasn't too long."

He was quiet, and the courtroom was quiet. The jury looked at one another and back to Teller.

The judge finally said to Sheila, "Do you wish to cross examine the witness?"

Sheila paused, looks at her assistant DAs who shake their heads, and says, "No questions, your honor."

Addressing Casey, the judge asks, "Mr. Casey, do you have any additional witnesses you wish to call?"

"No, your honor."

"Then this afternoon, we can have your closing statements. Court is adjourned until 2 p.m."

CHAPTER 68

———— ∽∾∽ ————

Brian leaves, to grab a bite of lunch, thinking about the testimony of Ed Teller. His first thought was the slogan that the radio commentator, Paul Harvey, used to say all the time, 'and now the other side of the story.' No one could listen to Teller without extending to him their sympathy for what he had lost. But, in the court of law, that didn't matter. He was guilty of murdering those children, and Brian was positive the jury would see it that way. The story and the pictures were too compelling to let their emotions dictate any result but guilty. He did wonder what effect Ed's statement, to the press and the families that lost their children, would have. It certainly was compelling. However, like Ed, he knew it probably would have little or no effect on the long-term crime rates in the Baltimore area.

Ironically, there was talk that Ed would be offered the opportunity to be part of a TV special on crime in the major cities of the US. At first, the DA and Brian were surprised that the media would consider Ed an authority on such matters but, then they realized that, what they thought didn't matter. The public would devour Teller's testimony because it was sensational. A real life reality show, with a multiple murderer as their star. Of course he'd have to do his part from a prison cell. Which, when you thought of it, was even more sensational. Personally, he was just happy that this trial was almost over. He needed to get back to his other duties, and stacks of paperwork, that required his attention. He never thought paperwork would seem so pleasant a thought.

The kids were bringing his granddaughter over this Sunday for brunch, and that brought a smile to his face. He and Sally felt like a young couple every time

Scott and Bridget let them babysit. Sally was spending more time with Andrew, running their auto repair and tire business. Scott was spending his time with the new Lake Drive project, helping Tony with the architects, and supervising the hiring of personnel for the development. Everyone was busy and, what was even better, they all seemed happy with what they were doing and accomplishing.

He walked to one of the food trucks, around the corner from the courthouse, grabbed a bite, and headed back to watch the final statement of the two opposing lawyers.

In the courthouse, Sheila had spent her lunch break going over her summation with her assistants. She has revised it several times, due to the lack of defense that Casey presented. At this point, she knows the jurors are anxious to be finished with this trial and go home to their families.

The court clerk yelled, "All rise," and the final act began.

Sheila's summation was simple and direct. She kept her voice low, and tried to show compassion for Mr. Teller at the outset. Then, she raised her voice enough to get the attention of the entire courtroom and said, "We can have compassion for Mr. Teller's loss. We can even understand his need to make a statement about his loss. But, can anyone," and she stopped and repeated "Can anyone condone the premeditated murder of six young children? This man, this killer, spent almost a year executing his plan to destroy the lives of not only these children, but their families as well. He's admitted this. He did not just kidnap and kill these children, he strangled them and placed plastic bags over their heads so they could not breathe. They all died in agony, unlike his son who was shot and killed with a single bullet, and who died instantly. No, this was not revenge as the bible describes 'an eye for an eye.' This was the worst kind of nightmare for these children. Frightened, alone, and in the hands of this maniac who describes himself as a good father. Using a Good Humor-style truck, to entice these children, is the worst part of it. They were innocents. They thought they were going to buy a treat, and instead they were led into his den of death."

"No, ladies and gentleman, this was nothing less than premeditated murder. That is what you need to remember, as you reach your verdict."

She walks over to the back of her table and pulls out the picture of the six dead children, with their heads wrapped in plastic, and brings it up to the jurors to see for the last time. "That is what this madman did to these children. He deserves to spend the rest of his life in a cell for what he did. I know you agree."

She turns away and heads to her table. Ron Casey continues to sit until she has taken her seat, then he begins to stand, only to have Ed grab his wrist. Ron turns and looks at Ed and asks, "What?" Ed, still holding his wrist, leans over to him and quietly says, "Enough. I've made my point. There really isn't any more to say, is there?"

Ron stares at Ed, seeing this once-dynamic executive that he met months ago, who has turned into this old man, whose hair is now fully gray, with matching complexion, and puts his hand over Ed's and says, "You're right. Of course, Ed. It's time to call it quits."

Ron stands and faces the judge and says, "We rest our case, your honor."

Sheila lets out a small sigh.

The judge, recognizing the impact this has on the jurors, begins immediately to instruct them how they will confer, and make their decision based on the facts of the case, as presented. And then he instructs them on their choices.

CHAPTER 69

As they file out, Sheila and her assistants collect their boxes of papers, and head out the door as the officer takes Ed back to his holding cell. Ron Casey sits at his table until most of the public has departed and then, lifting his attaché case with the paperwork from the trial, walks towards the exit. As he leaves the courtroom to await the verdict, he notices Brian Murphy standing alone in the corridor. He approaches him and says, "Your job on this case is done but, truthfully, has any more investigation taken place in regards to the killing of Teller's son?"

"Mr. Casey, having children of my own, I can't imagine what went through Teller's mind when he heard his son was killed by that stray bullet. However, as an officer of the law, which you fit into as well, I understand that whether or not the shooter was or is apprehended in the future, does not condone what Teller did to those children. The truth as I see it, and I have been thinking a lot about it, is that whatever the verdict is, Edward Teller has given away his right to freedom, whether he sits in a prison cell or at home in his living room, he will never be free again. He will never experience the joy of the life he had, and will always be haunted by the faces of those children. He is not some crazy sociopath. His conscience will catch up with him, and then God help him."

Casey puts out his hand to Brian and says, "You're a good cop, and a good man. I suspect we'll be seeing each other again."

Brian shakes his hand, then walks out of the courthouse.

The verdict, as predicted was anticlimactic. Guilty as charged, and sentenced to life imprisonment. The jurors filed out to face a horde of reporters and family waiting just outside the courthouse. Ed was quickly led through the courthouse corridors to the back door, where a van was waiting to convey him directly to prison. Since the area was fenced in, there were no reporters there, so getting him into the van, and headed out, took only a few minutes.

Two weeks after entering prison, Ed was taking a shower when three young men walked in and said to him, "This is a gift from Jack Hubbard and Manuel Diaz," and stabbed him to death. No weapon was ever discovered and no one was ever indicted for the murder.

CHAPTER 70

Five years had passed since Ed's death. The Lake Drive Murders, as they were still referred to, were all but forgotten by the public. The families who had lost their children would never forget, but their communities had moved on. The gangs still sold drugs and, although there were indeed fewer drive-by shootings, the new members of the gangs who were just six or seven when the crimes occurred, were now teenagers and were trying to make their mark in their gangs with guns.

Captain Brian Murphy, just a year from retirement, had become somewhat of a local hero for his part in not only bringing the murderer to justice, but what he had continued to do working with the inner-city gangs. He had persuaded the mayor and council to build a large sports facility, in the middle of the neighborhoods where the dead children had lived. And, with the help of the new 4 Baltimore Group, he was instrumental in the hiring of many of the youngsters into an apprentice program to teach them skills, for which they were being paid while they learned.

He and Terry were walking through the Lake Drive construction, looking at all the new condos and trees. They were heading towards a newly finished park that was to be used for the entire community, now covering 10 square blocks. In the center of the park was a large statue of six small children holding hands in a circle around a water fountain. It was dedicated, just this past weekend, with all the families of the murdered children invited to participate in the presentation.

The names of each of the children was etched into the base of the statue, as well the statement, "To Baltimore, with hope for the future."

As they reached the fountain, Brian turned to Terry and said, "Does any of this change the future?"

Terry thought for a moment, and answered, "I believe that change will occur slowly. It's inevitable that change happens. Will it be for the better? God, I hope so. So much suffering in these communities and, the only thing that will stop it, I believe, is more jobs and more education, neither of which has advanced much since the killings. The best thing that happened was the hiring of all these kids to help in the building of this new community. Hopefully, their pride in their work here will transfer to their own families, and that will be the start. A small one but, hell, anything is better than nothing."

Brian is looking at the statue, and remembering the pictures of the dead children with the plastic over their small heads and says, "Let's hope that these children's deaths end up having some impact. They deserve that, don't they?"

Made in the USA
Middletown, DE
05 December 2016